I0761703

STALKING THE DRAGON

Also by James Clay and available from Center Point Large Print:

The Justice Rider
Satan's Guns
Devil's Due
Gunfighter's Revenge
Songbird of the West

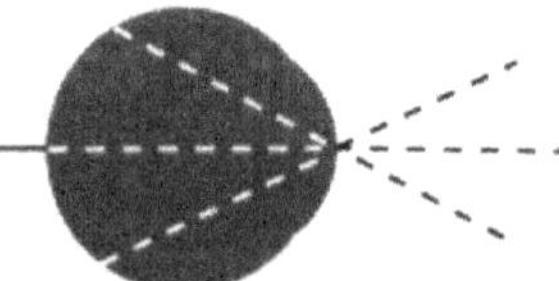

This Large Print Book carries the Seal of Approval of N.A.V.H.

STALKING THE DRAGON

JAMES CLAY

Center Point Large Print
Thorndike, Maine

This Center Point Large Print edition
is published in the year 2023 by arrangement with
the author.

The text of this Large Print edition is unabridged.
In other aspects, this book may vary
from the original edition.
Printed in the United States of America
on permanent paper sourced using
environmentally responsible foresting methods.
Set in 16-point Times New Roman type.

ISBN: 978-1-63808-596-6

The Library of Congress has cataloged this record
under Library of Congress Control Number: 2022946149

For Carol Ong-Chen who rides tall through the rugged plains of research

Chapter One

Kwok Meng watched the campfire carefully. Two years of mining for gold in California had taught him the danger of building a fire near trees. But Kwok was carrying a lot of money and he also knew the danger that came from the greed of men. He was camping out in a grove of trees where the light from the fire would be shielded.

After hanging a coffee can over the flames, he sat down and began to reread a letter from his wife, Choo, who was now calling herself Pearl. The woman was joyful. With the four hundred and fifty-seven dollars he was bringing back from his mining they could start a restaurant and make a fine life for themselves and their son.

Kwok smiled as he contemplated the future. He and his wife would not remain in San Francisco. They would find a nice town somewhere, a small town but not too small . . .

Kwok Meng's horse nickered and stomped a foot nervously. The young man's smile vanished. While folding the letter and putting it into his pocket, he listened carefully for sounds of an enemy. Approaching footsteps suddenly stopped. Or was that his imagination?

Kwok wasn't wearing a gun, but a Henry remained snugged in the boot of his saddle. Kwok pressed his lips in anger. He hadn't attended to his horse immediately as he should have done. The saddle was still on the buckskin, which was tied up several yards away.

Frightened, but still cautious and in control of himself, the man got to his feet and stepped toward his horse. A rifle shot shattered the quiet. A horrible burning pain seared through Kwok's body. He turned and saw a figure moving toward him: a figure that laughed as Kwok dropped to the ground.

Kwok's vision was blurred but he still recognized the figure that was suddenly standing over him. Kwok's voice was a tremulous whisper, "I trusted you . . ."

Another laugh, then the assailant set his rifle down and pulled out a knife.

Sheriff Deke Collins placed his drink down on the plank bar. He looked around the large tent and spotted nothing unusual: roulette wheels and chuck-a-luck cages were spinning, a few card games were going on and a scattering of gals in faded red and green dresses were trying to appear interested in the grizzled, defeated men that filled the tent.

The bartender, who was also the owner of Lester's Saloon, seemed to sense the lawman's mood. "I give this place another three months or so," he said as he filled Deke's glass. "Then I'm moving down to San Diego. Got enough money to open up a real saloon there."

"Yeh, the ground has pretty much given up what it's gonna give." Collins sipped his drink. "Some folks thought the gold strike here was like the ones back in the 1840's. Some folks were wrong. I think the war between the states had a hand in it. Men came outta the war restless and broke. So, they ended up coming to Rich Creek, hoping to find gold rocks just waiting to be picked up."

Lester had a bartender's instincts. He could spot what was really bothering a man. "Real shame 'bout that Kwok fella. Nice gent, never caused me no trouble, came in now and ag'in for a beer. He was a smart, hard workin' jasper, made himself a perty profit from that little vein he found. Sure didn't deserve to git shot like that."

"Yeh."

"But you nailed the killer, Sheriff!"

Collins' laugh was more of a scoff. "Weren't nothin' to it, the fool came to this here bar, got drunk and bragged on what he did. I almost carried him to the jailhouse. Confessed again when he sobered up."

"Ever give ya his real name?"

The lawman shook his head. "Jus' calls himself, 'Dragon.' "

The sheriff tried to laugh but couldn't manage it. His face twitched nervously. He dropped his voice to a whisper. "I tell ya, Lester, I'll be glad when the marshal gits here tomorra and hauls that Chinese cuss away. The look in that chink's eyes rakes right over my nerves. He's a strange one, all right. After shooting Meng in the back, he slashed his throat, jus' for fun."

Lester tried to hide his shock. Deke Collins had never before admitted to being scared, which he had just come close to doing. "Relax, the Dragon is in a cage!" The saloon owner tried to sound cheerful.

The sheriff looked edgy, not amused. "That man's body seems to be made of rubber. There are times I think he could slip right through the bars if he got a mind to."

Deke hastily gulped the drink in front of him and gave Lester a quick thanks. He left the tent and headed for the sheriff's office. The office was one of the few structures in Rich Creek not made of canvas. The town was really a settlement consisting primarily of tents.

As Collins stepped into the clapboard structure which served as the sheriff's office, he was assaulted by loud shouts in a language he couldn't understand. He clapped hands over his ears, but the screeches still stabbed through his head leaving a sharp pain.

"Shut up!" The lawman's order only caused the Dragon's voice to increase in power.

A sense of shame overwhelmed Deke Collins. He was allowing himself to be frightened—hell, terrified, by some little man with crazy eyes. The sheriff inhaled deeply and walked with a determined gait as he opened the door to the jail area.

U.S. Marshal Chet Benedict finished his meal: a hard task. The owner of Sally's Food Place noticed the grimace on her customer's face as he got up, tossed money onto the table, and headed for the exit. "We're closing down soon," she said to his back, trying to excuse the awful food.

"Good!" Chet left the tent and headed for the sheriff's office. He had never liked Rich Creek, even when the settlement seemed to be prospering. "A little bit of gold can drive a whole bunch of folks crazy," he said to himself.

Chet was a tall, beefy young man whose job made him sympathetic to the plight of Deke Collins. Deke had been a lawman most of his life. Now he was old, poor and in bad health. Still, he had managed to keep things orderly in the settlement. But what would happen to him when the tents were folded up and the dreamers gone?

Chet's mood was grim when he stepped into the office, which could have explained his immediate anxiety when he found the place deserted. "Sheriff?"

The marshal hadn't expected a reply and didn't get one. He quickly made his way through the door that led to the office's one jail cell.

Chet Benedict had seen many murder victims before in his young career, but never one with a cut throat. "Deke," he crouched over the body of the dead lawman, whose wide eyes stared at him from a head resting in a pool of dried blood. Collins' holster was empty. The cell door was open.

Benedict stood up, breathed deeply, and tried to quell the powerful emotions surging inside him. There was no doctor or undertaker in this God-forsaken place. He would have to see that Deke Collins received a Christian burial.

After that, he would talk to everyone left in Rich Creek. Find out what this buzzard called, "the Dragon," looked like. And then go after him.

Chet Benedict did just that. For three years he pursued the Dragon through a nightmarish trail of slashed throats. And then the killings stopped. Had the Dragon died, or vanished into the shadows, content with the death and sorrow he had inflicted on countless innocents?

That question pricked at the U.S. Marshal for several years. He followed a few leads that got him nowhere. Other cases came along, and Chet closed most of them. Chet Benedict got a well deserved reputation for being an outstanding lawman. The Dragon became an unpleasant memory which only plagued him occasionally.

But others did not forget at all.

Chapter Two

Fourteen Years Later

The noise in the Mule Kick Saloon subsided as Mack Wong walked inside and headed for the bar. He gave the bartender a polite smile, "I'd like a beer, please."

Jeb, the barkeep, appeared confused, as if the request was unusual. "Ah . . . sure, comin' up."

All eyes in the Mule Kick focused on the newcomer. Slightly less than average height, Mack Wong had rope-like muscles and a lithe body which moved with a natural grace.

Mack placed twenty five cents on the mahogany bar as Jeb plunked down a mug in front of him. After his customer had taken a sip of the brew, the barkeep spotted the burly form of Boone Witter moving his way. Trouble.

Witter halted at the far end of the bar. "Look at what some alley cat dragged in, a funny lookin' mouse," Boone laughed mockingly at Mack, who stood at the opposite end of the bar and appeared to not notice the insult.

"Boone, please—"

"Shut up, Jeb." Witter sniffed the air in an exaggerated manner. "All of a sudden, there's a rotten stink in this place, seems to be comin' from that place on the bar where that coolie put his hands. Barkeep, wipe that there spot clean."

Attempting to placate the troublemaker, Jeb grabbed a rag. He was stopped by a harsh stare from Mack Wong. Wong's voice was quiet but firm. "There is no need to clean."

Boone shouted loud enough to be heard outside in the street. "Say, I think we got a real important gent here tonight! I bet you're the Dragon, right, Chinaman?"

"I box under that name, yes."

"Yeh, I hear you're good with fists, how are ya with a gun, Chinaman?"

"I am not carrying a gun."

"Hell, we can fix that." Boone turned around to the nearest table behind him. "Rusty, let me borra your .44."

Rusty waved his hand in a friendly gesture, "Git back to your card game, Boone, I bet ya were winning—"

Boone took four steps toward the table where Rusty sat with one of the saloon girls. "Maybe ya didn't hear me sa good, I said give me your gun!"

Rusty hesitated. He and Boone Witter were sort of friends. They had worked at the same ranch for a few months. But Boone had gone from being a bit wild sometimes to a man who could quickly turn crazy and violent. A man who attacked the ramrod and got himself fired.

"I'm waitin'!"

"Okay, Boone." Rusty did what he had been told.

Witter's eyes burned with an intense hatred as he turned back toward the bar where now only one customer remained: Mack Wong.

"Come here, barkeep."

Jeb reluctantly obeyed the order. Boone handed him the .44. "I want ya to put the gun, real polite-like, in front of the Chinaman."

"Sure." The bartender grinned in a nervous, apologetic manner as he approached Mack and placed the gun in front of him. He then joined the customers who had left the bar but lined up around the saloon to enjoy the show.

Boone sauntered with a false casualness toward Mack Wong. His hand hovered over the Colt strapped to his waist. He suddenly stopped and scoffed before speaking. "I'm waitin', chink. Go for that gun any time you're ready."

"I have no argument with you." Mack's voice remained soft but could still be heard in the anxious silence which now gripped the saloon.

"Ya want an argument, do ya?" Boone took a step closer to his prey, his voice a shout. "I know ya Chinese put a lotta chips on ancestors. I know why ya call yourself 'the Dragon.' Well, it won't do no good. Your ancestors is nothin' more than a bunch of snakes!"

Mack Wong tried to calm his anger as he stared at the gun in front of him.

• • •

"I have never understood the emphasis Asians place on family," Stacey Hooper's voice was buoyant. He and his companion were approaching Grayson, Texas. A long ride was almost over. "Of course, I am a dubious source to be commenting on such matters. My family . . . ah . . . strongly encouraged me to leave England and start a new life in America. Or any other place that was far away."

"My job is not to understand Mack Wong, but to protect him," Rance Dehner explained. "His uncle, Sammy Wong, knows me from a previous case I had in Grayson. Sammy thinks his nephew may be in danger."

Stacey sounded amused. "I'd say that is rather apparent. Anyone who is scheduled to fight Bruiser Bill Connors is obviously in danger."

Dehner shook his head. "No, it's not the boxing aspect. Something else has Sammy worried and he thinks a detective might help. That's why he contacted me at the Lowrie Agency."

"Does it have anything to do with this crazy notion Mack has of compensating for the sins of his father?"

"Maybe. Mack has taken the name of 'the Dragon,' the name his father used when he cut the throats of at least five people. We'll never know how many murders could be laid at the feet of the Dragon."

"But, from what I understand, Mack never met his father, at least not when he was at an age to remember him."

"True enough," Dehner assented. "But some rumors claim the Dragon disappeared into the Chinese district of San Franscisco. That's where Mack and most of his family lives. Maybe Mack figures hiding dad became a family affair."

"And that's why Mack donates a big chunk of his winnings to charitable endeavors."

"Yep!" Dehner replied. "The money he makes off his fight with Bruiser Bill will go to help build a clinic in Grayson."

The two men rode past Delilah's, the whorehouse being the first commercial establishment on Grayson's Main Street. As they slowly plodded on, Dehner looked around, reacquainting himself with the layout of the town. "Look for Sammy's Hotel and Restaurant, we're—"

A loud, angry voice fired like a bullet from a nearby saloon. "I know why ya call yourself 'the Dragon.' Well, it won't do no good. Your ancestors is nothin' more than a bunch of snakes!"

"Watch the horses, Stacey! I better start earning my pay!" Dehner did a fast slide off his horse and ran toward the Mule Kick Saloon.

Chapter Three

Rance stopped at the saloon's batwings and looked over the situation. A man who had to be Mack Wong was standing at the bar. He betrayed no emotion as he looked at a man whose red face bristled with hate.

"Let it alone, Boone!" Someone shouted from inside the Mule Kick.

"No! I'm sick of the way his kind is takin' over." Boone Witter began to breathe deeply and quickly. His eyes were becoming glassy. "We got a chink fer mayor and he owns half the town. Now, he's bringin' his nephew here to play the big hero. Well, let him prove he's a hero!"

"Evening, gents!" Dehner strolled into the Mule Kick beaming an absurd smile. "I'm from the Citizens Civility Committee."

"What the—" Witter mumbled.

Rance continued to smile as he approached Boone. "Our committee believes in settling disputes without guns. So, we offer our special services." The detective began to unstrap the gun belt which held the holster containing his Colt. "I will gladly fight you with fists. Toss down your gun and I'll even let you throw the first punch."

"Ya must be crazy—"

Dehner swung his gun belt. The Colt slammed

into Witter's mouth. Boone's head snapped sideways and Rance followed with a fast punch to the head. Boone Witter fell to the floor, dazed but conscious.

Rance grabbed his adversary's pistol as he laid his own gun belt over his shoulder. He grabbed Boone's arm, pulled him up, and walked him out of the saloon. Stacey Hooper was waiting outside. "I've been watching closely, in the event you needed assistance."

Rance handed Stacey Boone's gun. "Could you help our friend to stay upright for a moment?" Dehner continued to speak as he strapped his gun belt back on. "As I recall, the sheriff's office is less than a ten minute walk. The mayor told me that Grayson now has different lawmen than when I was last in town. Witter, you and I are going to meet the new sheriff and deputy together."

"I ain't goin' to no—"

"Don't be so contrary, Boone, you're about to get a comfortable place to sleep tonight at no expense." Hooper's voice continued to sound merry. "And Rance, you have gotten an excellent start on your assignment. I'm sure high praises will soon come your way."

"Maybe not," Dehner replied. "I don't think Mack Wong was very happy with someone cutting in and taking over his battle. I have a feeling he's going to let me know all about that very soon."

Chapter Four

Rance Dehner was overwhelmed by the many oddities of the meeting. Sammy Wong was the mayor of Grayson. While there were a large number of Chinese in the West, few had run for, never mind attained, political office.

Sammy sat in the living room of his home, which was one of the finest in the town. He was presiding over a meeting in a large comfortable armchair. Rance sat beside Sammy on a comfortable but smaller chair. Stacey was seated beside Rance.

Sitting across and several feet away from Sammy was his sister-in-law, Wai Lan, the mother of Mack. Wai was a lovely woman of indeterminate age. She was thin and sat with perfect posture.

The rest of the participants were scattered about in a bent circle consisting of chairs of varying sizes. Mack and Jenny, Sammy's daughter of nineteen years, sat beside each other. Also seated side by side were Barry and Peter Thomas. Barry Thomas owned the gym in San Francisco where Mack trained. Barry was a man whose appearance left no doubt he had once been a boxer. His face appeared hammered, and his ears had absorbed more than a few too many beatings. Otherwise, he was in good condition, the rest of his body reflecting the long hours spent in his own gym. Salt was starting to get the advantage in his salt and pepper hair.

Barry Thomas was Mack's trainer. The status of his son, Peter, was vague. Peter appeared to be in his early twenties with brown hair and a handsome face which showed few signs of battle. Like his father, he could be a good advertisement for Thomas' Gym and Boxing Club, but there was an unease to Peter's demeanor. He appeared anxious that he might be asked to justify his presence and find himself unable to respond.

After the introductions were over, Mack spoke to his uncle. "Uncle, you have been very kind to me since I arrived from San Francisco yesterday. And I deeply appreciate the help Mr. Dehner provided for me this evening. But it was unnecessary. I do not require a babysitter."

Sammy glared at his nephew in a manner that injected more fear into the young man than any opponent he had encountered in the ring. "Mr. Dehner is not your babysitter. There are matters about fight with Bill Connors of which you know nothing. You will cooperate with Mr. Dehner."

"Yes, Uncle."

Sammy turned to Rance Dehner. "One good thing about Asian family, it is easy for old man to pull rank."

Dehner, Stacey Hooper and the Thomas duo

laughed at the quip. Sammy's family members all smiled politely.

Sammy continued: "At recommendation of Mr. Dehner, I have also employed services of Mr. Stacey Hooper. Mr. Hooper is professional gambler, who, I understand, has assisted Mr. Dehner in some detective work. Stacey Hooper will oversee taking bets on fight. Of course, we cannot control all the gambling. But Mule Kick Saloon will be official site where men can place bets on the fight. Background and integrity of Mr. Hooper will ensure process is carried out with utmost honesty."

Sammy smiled and nodded in Stacey's direction. Hooper's face beamed at the patriarch's compliments. Rance noticed that the other occupants in the room didn't seem to completely share Sammy's confidence.

Sensing the unease, Jenny spoke up. Her voice carried a musical quality. "Father, are you still planning on a special welcoming for Mr. Connors tomorrow?"

"Yes," Sammy responded. "Mr. Connors arrives on noon stagecoach. He will stay at my hotel. He will be guest in our home in the evening. Following evening meal, we will go to church for Wednesday night prayer meeting. There, we say prayers no one get serious injury in fight."

All this was a bit much for Barry Thomas. "Mr. Wong, I believe in being a good sport and all, but having two boxers together like that, in a church no less, just a few days before they fight, ain't a good idea."

"I am sure you are correct regarding most boxing matches, Mr. Thomas. But this match is special. My nephew already donated his share of profits to establishment of a medical clinic in Grayson. The clinic will serve not only town of Grayson, but many surrounding towns and communities. Therefore, events I have spoken of are quite appropriate. Now, I must meet in private with Mr. Dehner and his associate. I wish you all very pleasant night."

The mayor's eyes became mischievous as he stood up. "For those who do not get hint, I no longer like you here. Otherwise, do as you wish."

Rance and Stacey got up and began to follow Sammy. Dehner quickly ran his eyes over the others in the room. The detective was not surprised that Peter Thomas was glancing at Jenny Wong. Jenny had long black hair framing an oval face with a mouth that always seemed to be smiling. Right now, she was smiling back at her admirer. Lucky guy.

Sammy guided his guests down a short hallway, then stopped, opened a door, and smiled graciously as he motioned them inside. The smile vanished when he closed the door and walked toward a large desk, opened the top drawer, and pulled out a piece of paper.

"I received this less than honorable communication last week."

Rance took the paper. Words cut from a newspaper and pasted to the paper read, "death to the Dragon." Under the words were a drawing of Mack Wong also taken from the newspaper. The drawing showed Mack from the waist up, holding his fists in a typical boxer pose. A slash of red ink ran across his throat.

"Was this sent through the mail?" Dehner asked.

"No. I was working at the hotel desk last Tuesday. And, like always, at ten A.M. I went into restaurant area to make sure all was going well in preparation for lunch. When I return, I find envelope with my name on it. This note inside."

"Your name on the envelope, was it also clipped from a newspaper?" Dehner asked.

Sammy nodded his head. "I'm sure all words and picture clipped from same newspaper article about Dragon, comc to Grayson to fight Bruiser Bill. Our criminal is wise with money. Only have to invest a lousy two cents for one copy of the *Grayson Herald*."

Dehner lowered his voice as if telling an off-color joke. "Sammy, I don't like bringing this up but—"

"We must not be delicate!" Sammy interrupted. "Some people in Grayson hate Asians. This bccome quite evident in race for mayor."

Stacey looked confused. "But you won the election!"

"Yes, most citizens of Grayson recognize outstanding leadership qualities of humble self." The mayor chuckled, as he always did when saying, *humble self*. "But Sammy's opponent good politician. Claim fact that Sammy Chinese not to count in election. At same time, he speak of shifty eyed oriental."

"This gent would do well in Chicago," Dehner said. "What's his name?"

"Bo Kendrick, he owns gun shop."

"How many votes did you win the election by?" Dehner asked.

"Twenty-two. Most people like Sammy. Compliment him on food in restaurant. Sammy not tell . . . someone else do cooking!"

Dehner chuckled and shook his head. Sammy Wong enjoyed employing humor. He made fun of how Americans viewed Asians and vice-versa. But the jokes often made it difficult to understand what the man was really thinking. Of course, Dehner mused, that could be exactly what Sammy wanted.

"Allow me to move the discussion off politics for the moment," Stacey said. "How did this boxing match between Mack Wong: the Dragon, and Bruiser Bill come about?"

The mayor smiled but his eyes turned sad. "Mack wish to make up for what preacher call the ‘sins of his father.’ Mack proud when Uncle elected mayor. He wants to help with clinic.”

Stacey pressed on. “How did Bruiser Bill get involved?”

“Sammy, in his capacity as mayor, get notice from Mr. Connors’ agent, Roscoe Platt. Mr. Platt inform that Bruiser Bill on tour of West, fighting best fighter town can produce. Mr. Connors charge thirty-five dollars for this service, plus fifteen per cent of ticket sales. Rest of money will go to town.”

Rance was surprised by the look of sadness on Stacey Hooper’s face. Not much saddened Stacey, but the regret was apparent in the Brit’s voice. “Only a few years ago, Bruiser Bill Connors was the top boxer in this country. Now he’s doing a humiliating tour, fighting anyone for thirty-five dollars up front.”

The detective crunched his face in confusion. “Mack Wong is a serious boxer. How did Roscoe Platt respond when you informed him about your nephew, Sammy?”

“He agree to fight. As old American expression go, ‘dollar is dollar.’ ”

Rance tugged his ear, then asked, “How is the medical clinic coming along?”

“Okay, but can use more money,” Sammy replied. “Clinic now headed by Doctor Edward Ackerman. Do not call him, ‘Eddie.’ Another doctor arrive next week to care for Grayson.

Dr. Ackerman plan to travel about to ranches, towns and new settlements."

Rance nodded his head. "Was the clinic your idea?"

"No, no, clinic is dream of Doctor Fred Cranston."

Dehner smiled broadly. "I remember Doc Cranston, look forward to seeing him again."

"Oh. Afraid not possible."

"Why?" Dehner asked.

"Last week, Doctor Fred Cranston murdered."

Chapter Five

Sheriff Cal Markham looked with curiosity at the man walking beside him. Scoop Wilsey was scribbling in a notebook as he asked questions. There wasn't much of a moon above and only a few stars. The man must have good eyes.

"So, Sheriff, you still have no idea who killed Doc Cranston?"

"No, but I got the facts nailed. Doc had breakfast that mornin' at Sammy's Hotel and Restaurant. He tole folks there he was gonna visit sick people at two ranches that day. Both ranches are big and Doc said the owners had promised him a donation for the clinic. I checked both places and sure enough they gave Doc Cranston money for the clinic along with payin' him for patchin' 'em up."

"So you belicvc robbery was the motive?"

"Yeh . . ." The sheriff didn't seem too confident in his own statement.

Wilsey's mind briefly went over the discovery of the doctor's corpse. Eight nights back, the familiar sight of Doctor Cranston's buggy had been making its way slowly through town. Scoop Wilsey was the first to notice the contraption was empty. He ran to inform the sheriff, and the two men rode out in search of the doctor.

They found him in less than an hour. Doctor Fred Cranston had been shot twice, his corpse left at the side of a road leading into town. No blood was found inside the buggy, so Doctor Cranston had apparently been ordered onto the road and robbed before being murdered.

Markham stopped in front of a hardware store. The lawman checked the door, making sure it was locked, then did the same for the barber shop next to it. The two men then continued down the boardwalk.

Scoop had to look up as he questioned the lawman. The newspaper owner stood at slightly less than average height. Cal Markham was six feet with a craggy face and reddish-blond hair. Both men were in their mid-twenties.

"But if all they wanted was money, why not just rob Doc Cranston, instead of killing him?"

Across the street, loud shouts emanated from the Lucky Trail Saloon accompanied by an out of tune piano. Markham stopped and lowered his voice before answering Wilsey's question. " 'Cause whoever done it figgered Doc recognized him. I'm keepin' an eye out for any jasper spendin' more money than he's got a right to have. I'd sure appreciate it if you'd not put that last point in the newspaper."

Scoop nodded his head. "Sure. Say, are you and your deputy ready for the big boxing match?"

The sheriff looked at the sky and gave a

humorless laugh. "This town is already goin' a bit crazy. But Buck and me can handle—"

A sound of broken glass and loud curses shot out of the Lucky Trail. "I better git over there," the lawman nodded a quick goodbye and headed for the saloon.

Before entering the Lucky Trail, Markham looked back and saw Scoop stuffing his notebook and pencil into the pocket of his jacket as he walked back to the *Herald* office. He didn't know exactly how the newspaperman had picked up the nickname, "Scoop", but did know Wilsey's real first name was "Phineas."

"With a name like that, guess you'd grab any nickname folks would give ya," he whispered.

A drunken cowhand fired a bullet into the ceiling of the Lucky Trail. Cal Markham plowed through the batwings to restore peace.

Scoop walked slowly, feeling more than a bit ashamed of himself. Doctor Fred Cranston had done so much for Grayson, Texas. Over the last year, he had brought another doctor into the town and they had been working at establishing a clinic. He had even arranged for the third doctor, who would be arriving with his wife next week. The hunt for Doc Cranston's killer should be the top story in every edition of the *Grayson Herald.*

But the whole town was caught up in the

excitement of a fight between Mack Wong: the Dragon, and Bruiser Bill Connors. And Scoop was caught up more than anyone for reasons beyond an interest in the sport of boxing.

Dozens of newspapers across the country had contacted him about using his coverage of the fight. As he stepped off one boardwalk Scoop mused happily to himself that his stuff would be read by hundreds of people, maybe thousands! He heard a rustling sound but didn't see the attacker who grabbed his arm and flung him into an alley.

Surrounded by darkness, Scoop could barely make out the attacker who quickly advanced on him. Something hard slammed against Wilsey's head. The reporter hit the ground, seeing red. Next, he saw a gun barrel pressed between his eyes. Above the gun was a figure wearing a black hood.

"I gotta story for ya, newspaper guy."

"Ye . . . s . . ." came the semi-conscious reply.

"There's a lot o' us in this town that thinks we already got enough Chinese."

The voice sounded unnaturally low. Scoop wondered if Black Hood felt compelled to disguise it.

The low growl continued. "We don't want no Dragon in our town. If Mack Wong fights Bill Connors, he dies. Put that on your front page."

The figure stood up and vanished. Wilsey thought he heard footsteps running off but couldn't be sure. Scoop gradually got back onto his feet. But he couldn't stay there. The world was so dark, he wasn't sure which way to go. Then the ground began to spin and he once more collided with it.

Doctor Edward Ackerman handed Scoop a glass. "Drink this, you need water."

The newspaperman felt self-conscious. People surrounded him with sympathetic stares as he sat propped up in a bed in the doctor's surgery.

When Scoop had been late getting back to the modest edifice that housed the *Grayson Herald*, his wife, Mandy, had gone to the sheriff's office. Rance Dehner and Stacey Hooper were there talking with the sheriff and his deputy, Buck, about the upcoming boxing match. Mandy knew Rance from the previous case he had investigated in Grayson.

"Ma'am, it's been more than an hour since I jawed with your husband," Cal spoke in response to a question by Mandy. "He was walkin' back to his office last I saw him." The lawman couldn't miss the worried look on the woman's face. "We got us five people right here, I bet we'll find that husband of yours in no time."

No time was about twenty-five minutes. Buck, a sixtyish man with fluffs of white hair sticking to his head and a gimp in one leg located Scoop moaning in the alley. The reporter could only get to his feet with help.

After drinking his water, Wilsey relayed what little information he could regarding the assault.

"So, ya can't tell us nothin' 'bout this buzzard who beat ya up?"

"I'm afraid not, Buck, he seemed to be trying to disguise his voice, that's all I can say."

Mandy wrapped an arm around her husband's shoulder. "Can he go home tonight, Doctor?"

"Yes, as long as . . ."

While Doctor Ackerman gave the usual advice about taking care, Rance Dehner tried to assess the situation. Ackerman impressed him as unusual for a western doctor. Most of the docs he had encountered were older men or young idealists. Ackerman stood outside the mold. He appeared to be in his mid-thirties, his dark hair and mustache not revealing a trace of gray.

During his last visit, Dehner had envied Scoop Wilsey, and still did. Wilsey had a meaningful job and a beautiful wife to help him run the *Grayson Herald*. And Mandy was more than beautiful, she was a very special lady who deeply loved her husband. Dehner wondered why he couldn't have . . .

The detective silently chastised himself. Envying others and wallowing in self-pity was a bad horse to mount.

Scoop agreed to most of what the doctor instructed but hastily added, “Tomorrow I have to be there when the noon stage arrives—the stage bringing Bruiser Bill Connors!”

Chapter Six

About fifty people were scattered on the boardwalk in front of the stage depot as noon approached. Among the fifty were all the members of the Wong family. Sammy had assembled them to be an official greeting party for Bruiser Bill.

"Too bad Bill arrive on Wednesday," Sammy commented to Rance and Stacey, who stood on one side of the mayor. "Many townspeople here, but ranchers and ranch hands must stay on ranch. Duty before pleasure."

Mack was on the other side of Sammy from Rance and Stacey. Scoop and Mandy Wilsey stood close by, accompanied by their small but energetic dog, Clyde. Clyde's tail was wagging, and he occasionally barked, obviously aware that something exciting was going on. Scoop's face was pale and his head bandaged, but his enthusiasm remained unchecked. He was almost as excited as his dog. He anxiously asked Grayson's mayor, "Why was there no reception like this for the Dragon?"

A mischievous smile creased Sammy's wide face. "Honorable nephew ahead of Bruiser Bill in achieving virtue of humility."

The stage clattered in only twenty minutes late.

Neither the driver nor the shotgun were surprised by the crowd. "We got two passengers for you, Sammy," the driver shouted good naturedly.

The good nature ended abruptly. A short, bald headed man dressed in an expensive suit jumped out of the stage and began to shout as his feet hit the ground. "What the hell is this?" He pointed an angry finger at Sammy, Mack and the rest of their family who were now lined up behind them. "Looks to me like all of Chinatown in San Francisco came down here to start an opium den!"

A stunned silence followed. Even Clyde remained still, wondering whether he should growl. This was not what anyone was expecting. Stacey Hooper smiled broadly as he placed a hand on the newcomer's shoulder and addressed the crowd in the manner of Brutus' speech to the Romans. "Citizens of Grayson, we are blessed to have in our midst, Mr. Roscoe Platt! Mr. Platt is a student of the sweet science of boxing, though he has never actually stepped into the ring himself."

Roscoe looked irritated. He obviously found Stacey's interruption of his vitriol to be rude. "Whatta you doing here, Limey? I remember you from Denver, you helped set up the betting for—"

Stacey quickly cut in. "We won't bore these fine people with our reminisces, Roscoe." Hooper took his hand off Platt's shoulder and held it up to indicate important information was about to be conveyed. “Roscoe Platt is not only an authority on the sport of boxing, he’s a staunch believer in doing anything for publicity. There is no individual or group under the canopy of heaven Roscoe won’t insult in order to get a couple of lines in a newspaper.”

A voice sounded from inside the stagecoach. “That’s tellin’ ’em, Hooper!”

“There he is!” and similar shouts fired from the crowd as Bruiser Bill Connors stepped from the stagecoach.

“Ain’t seen you since Denver, Stacey.” Everything about Bruiser Bill Connors was huge. He stood at close to six and a half feet. Connors’ voice boomed. Boom seemed to be its natural level. “As I recall, Hooper, you were part of the gang I had dinner with after my fight with Kid Hansen. I think it was a week or two before the kid was able to eat anything solid.”

Having made his point, Bill took off his Stetson revealing thick, sandy colored hair. He respectfully extended his hand to the official host. “You must be Mayor Wong. Real nice to meet you.”

“Welcome to Grayson, Mr. Connors. I would like to introduce you to your honorable opponent, my nephew, Mack Wong.”

Bruiser Bill’s movements slowed down. He gave Mack a careful assessment. Shaking Mack’s hand was a drawn out affair. Connors spoke to his opponent, but his words were primarily for the crowd. "Good luck, Mack . . . but not too much luck."

As people laughed, Mandy Wilsey whispered to her husband, "Bruiser's arms look like tree trunks."

Scoop nodded agreement before whispering back, "And they are long. I don't see how Mack can get near him."

While the introductions had been going on, Roscoe Platt had ignited a cigar. He now waved the stogie in the air to refocus attention on himself. "Folks, Bruiser Bill Connors wants to meet ever one of the fine citizens of Grayson. He will be in the lobby of the . . . ah . . ."

The mayor helped out in a quiet voice, "Sammy's Hotel and Restaurant."

"Sammy's Hotel and chow place tomorra afternoon from three to six P.M. He'll be signing autographs for only twenty-five cents—ten cents for children under twelve. You gotta bring the whole family fer a once in a lifetime chance to meet Bruiser Bill Connors in person!"

Sammy Wong's face went gray. He hadn't been informed about Bruiser Bill signing autographs for money and the announcement didn't make him happy. But he forced a smile across his countenance and led Bill and Roscoe to the Hotel.

Dehner and Hooper followed the procession

along with several stragglers. “I didn’t know you had worked with Roscoe and Bill Connors in Denver, Stacey?” Dehner’s voice made the statement a question.

Hooper waved his arm indicating the whole matter was insignificant. “Yes, there were some problems with how the betting was being handled. I served as a consultant.”

“You didn’t tell me about this!”

Stacey shrugged his shoulders. “Of course not, you know me well enough to understand I share Mack Wong’s gift of humility.”

Dehner responded with a caustic laugh. Stacey looked amused.

Chapter Seven

Jeb Smith looked over the large number of people crowding into the Grayson Community Church. "Never seen so many people in a Wednesday night prayer meetin' before, Preacher Paul. Some folks will jus' have ta stand up."

The smile on Paul Colten's face had nothing to do with the large attendance. He liked the name Preacher Paul. It was a welcome change from Reverend Colt, the name he had carried as a gunfighter.

"Looks like you'll be in for a busy night at the Mule Kick, Jeb. I know a lot of the men folk won't be heading directly home after the meeting."

Jeb looked at the floor as he laughed. "My momma woulda' been proud of me bein' in church, but bein' the head barkeep at the Mule Kick? Reckon she wouldn't a' fancied that so much."

Colten patted Jeb Smith on the shoulder, then stepped onto the platform and behind a pulpit. He looked to his left where Mandy Wilsey sat at a piano and nodded that she was ready.

After opening with a prayer, Colten declared, "We have a large group here tonight, let's lift our voices to heaven. Mandy, how do we start?"

"Amazing Grace."

Fifteen minutes later, the pastor commended the congregation on their enthusiastic singing. "We have a lot of people here tonight and I know why. This is a special week for Grayson. We have two outstanding athletes in our midst who will meet each other in the ring this Saturday at noon. As some of you know, I did a little boxing myself back East in my college days, so they have asked me to referee. It's always reassuring for a preacher to know people trust him with an important job."

A modest degree of laughter tingled in the church. Paul Colten continued: "I am going to ask Mr. Bill Connors and Mr. Mack Wong to please stand up."

Both fighters complied with the preacher's request. They were sitting on opposite ends of the same front pew. They had arrived together from the dinner at Sammy's home. Bruiser Bill smiled and waved at the crowd. Mack looked uncomfortable. His eyes remained straight ahead.

"I am going to ask you gentlemen to be so kind as to say a few words." Colten gestured toward Mack, "Mr. Wong."

"I am very grateful for the welcome I have received in Grayson."

"Thank you, Mr. Wong, Mr. Bru-, Mr. Connors, would you like to say something?"

"I sure would, Preacher!" As always, Connors'

voice boomed. "This is a swell town, you've sure welcomed this boy from a hardscrabble farm!"

Bill clasped his hands together and held them high as cheers came from some of the assembled. "And Mack, you sure got yourself a humdinger of a family. Why, your uncle owns the hotel and restaurant, the livery, and most important, the Mule Kick Saloon. All my uncle owns is a broken down still and he makes me pay for his lousy rot gut."

Laughter resounded through the church. Connors waited for it to subside and then continued as he looked directly at Mack. "I guess you got more book learnin' than me. I hear you wanna fight according to the mar-keys somethin'."

Mack nodded his head in a manner that was almost a bow. "The Marquess of Queensbury Rules are the rules of modern boxing."

"That's what I hear," Bruiser Bill shot back. "This here mar-keys says boxers should wear gloves. Guess I'm old fashioned, I thought gloves was what you wore when it got cold."

Loud laughter exploded again. Preacher Paul grimaced. This wasn't the good sportsmen exchange he had been expecting.

Mack Wong's face remained expressionless. "Mr. Connors, you are an acclaimed and accomplished boxer. I am honored to step into the ring with you. If you wish, we will fight without gloves."

"Isn't bare knuckle boxing illegal?" Mandy blurted out.

Sounds of confusion came from the congregation. People seemed to sense something important had just happened, but they didn't know exactly what.

Mandy gave Preacher Paul a chagrinned smile as if apologizing for her outburst. Paul shook his head, absolving her of guilt. He was privately chastising himself for asking the two boxers to talk. Well, it had seemed like a good idea.

"Thank you, Mr. Connors and Mr. Wong. I think that now . . . ah . . . now is a time for prayer."

Chapter Eight

Mack Wong looked at himself in the mirror as he removed the tie he had worn to church that evening. His thoughts were on Bill Connors. The young fighter was becoming increasingly certain his suspicions about Bruiser Bill were correct.

"Mack, it's Barry," both the voice and the knock on the door that accompanied it sounded angry.

The trainer entered the room before Mack could say anything. "I thought you were smart!" Barry Thomas paced about the guest bedroom in the Wong home. "Why'd ya let Connors get the best of ya this evening?!"

"You must be referring to my agreement to fight Mr. Connors bare knuckle."

"Hell yes, that's what I mean! Didn't ya see the way Connors looked ya over at the stage depot? He spotted your weakness. You've got strong arms but the power has to be delivered by those small hands of yours. Ya hurt just one of those hands in the fight and Bruiser Bill will turn ya into a bloody puddle."

"I feel con—"

Barry hadn't finished venting. "Besides, that gal at the piana was right. Bare knuckle boxing is illegal!"

"The sport of boxing is illegal in many places. No one cares or pays attention."

Barry Thomas fell silent, but he continued to pace about the room. He stopped, sighed deeply, and then changed the subject. "Have ya seen that son of mine since we got past the praying?"

"No. Can't you locate him?"

"I sure can't but I got me an idea what he's up ta and I don't like it."

Preacher Paul was suspicious the moment Jenny Wong and Peter Thomas approached him after the prayer meeting. Jenny told the pastor that Peter was interested in Paul's journey from being a clergyman to being a gunfighter to returning to being a man of the cloth.

Even a concise summary of those events took time. When Paul had finished, everyone had departed the church except the young couple. This, of course, necessitated that Peter walk Jenny home.

Preacher Paul laughed as he watched the couple leave the church. "Wonder if I will be performing a wedding any time soon."

Outside the church, Jenny began their walk and conversation with a compliment. "Mack Wong is very fortunate to have two such fine trainers as you and your father."

"I'm not a trainer. Oh, I know boxing well enough to serve as a second for Mack."

"What is a second?"

Peter shrugged his shoulders to indicate the unimportance of his job. "Between the rounds of a match, I wipe the sweat off Mack and tend any wounds as best as I can. I did some boxing in the army. Didn't amount to much. Army life can get pretty dull at times. Guys hold boxing matches as a way of passing time."

They turned right as they reached an area between the church and the commercial area of the town. In front of them was a long double line of homes. That the Wong home was the last in one of those lines pleased Peter. He wanted to impress the young lady and realized he was getting off to a bad start.

"Did you enjoy army life?" Jenny asked.

"I only joined because I didn't know what else to do with myself." Peter inwardly cursed his honesty, then added truthfully, "But I did learn a lot about guns and horses, especially horses, which can come in handy."

"Yes, certainly that is true."

Both Peter and Jenny fidgeted nervously as they neared the Wong home. "It's a beautiful night." Peter was lying and they both knew it. The moon was little more than a slight, misty smudge. Not a star dotted the sky. "Why don't we walk along the road for a spell. I'd like to see more of Grayson."

Jenny spotted the figure of Auntie Wai Lan

appearing in a window of the Wong house. Auntie Wai Lan was expressionless and yet somehow condemning.

Jenny turned her head and viewed the "more of Grayson" Peter had been talking about. A road, wide enough to perhaps accommodate a buggy, ran across flat ground for a half mile before it cut into a grove of emaciated trees. "Yes, it . . . is a lovely evening."

As they continued their walk, Peter remembered hearing one of his army buddies telling him women loved to talk about themselves. He wasn't sure his friend knew any Asian females but hoped the statement applied across the board. "You and your father have sure done a lot in this town. I mean owning the hotel, saloon and . . ."

"My father is the one who has done so much."

Jenny realized she had cut off Peter's awkward attempt at conversation. She tried again. "My father, even as mayor, has limitations to his business interests."

The road was becoming increasingly rocky. Peter kicked a small stone a few yards down the road. "I don't understand."

"The economy of Grayson is built on ranching. My father is learning everything he can about how to run a ranch. But there is much he still . . ."

Jenny stumbled and Peter grabbed her. They

stared at each other for a moment, then the lady straightened up as Peter let go.

"Thank you, Mr. Thomas."

"Ah, please call me Peter."

"Peter! And you may call me Jenny."

"Jenny!" Peter's voice resounded with triumph. He quickly lowered it. "This road is getting pretty rough. Maybe we better start back."

"Yes."

Peter, encouraged by the success his quick reflexes had brought, became a tad more inquisitive. "Chinese often run laundries. I notice there isn't one here in Grayson."

He immediately regretted the question. Even in the dark, he could tell his companion looked uncomfortable.

"In San Francisco and other cities, Chinese laundries have become locations for opium dens," Jenny explained. "My father has witnessed the terrible destruction these places bring. However, Grayson will have a Chinese laundry soon. It will be run by people my father trusts deeply. My two cousins: they will arrive tomorrow."

"Sounds like your father sure has strong feelings when it comes to drugs."

"Yes. He keeps in touch with Tom Bascomb, who runs Bascomb's Emporium. He sells opium, laudanum, and morphine in small supplies. Mr. Bascomb shares my father's concerns. If he notices a customer buying too many drugs, he reports it to Doctor Ackerman, who investigates immediately. Sometimes, the sheriff has to get involved."

As they returned to the Wong home, Peter tried to break the somber mood he had unintentionally invoked. "Say, I'll be working up an appetite tomorrow morning, running and exercising with Mack. Come noon, I'll be hungry. It sure would pleasure me if you'd join me for lunch."

Jenny laughed softly. "I'm in charge of my father's restaurant. I will be getting my exercise serving you and Mack your food."

"Oh . . . I forgot . . ."

"Do you like tea?"

"Yes!" Peter replied while trying to remember the last time he had drunk the stuff.

"I usually relax with a cup of tea at the restaurant around two o' clock in the afternoon. Would you like to join me then?"

"I sure would!" They were now standing in front of the Wong home. Peter felt he should come up with some poetic way of saying good night but his excitement over being asked to tea made him nervous, not eloquent. "Well, sleep good, ah, I'll meet you tomorrow for tea."

"Peter?"

The young man looked at the lady anxiously. "Yes?"

"If you wish, you may have coffee or sarsaparilla while I drink my tea."

“Thanks.” Peter stood and watched as Jenny walked to the front door of the house. In the process, she waved to her aunt, who had once again found her way to a front window.

Auntie Wai Lan moved her head slightly in reply, which bothered Jenny, but Peter didn’t notice. Music filled the young man’s soul as he made his way to Sammy’s Hotel and Restaurant. He would be sleeping in the place where Jenny worked, and her father owned. In a way, he would be close to her.

Giddiness triggered by a beautiful young woman kept Peter Thomas from spotting the threat which had been trailing behind him since he and Jenny left the church. The figure remained several yards behind his prey, curtained by the darkness. The stalker had taken refuge behind a scrawny tree when the couple turned around. It was the only cover he needed in the black of night. He continued his stalking as Thomas proceeded by himself but paused as his target reached the kerosene lamps of Grayson’s Main Street. The stalker whispered ugly oaths, threatening two people who, in his eyes, were acting indecently, brazenly defying the laws of nature. They would soon pay the penalty.

Chapter Nine

Preacher Paul Colten awoke suddenly and gazed around the church office, which also served as his bedroom. The office boasted one small window which on this night offered almost no light. Instinctively, he figured the time to be about one A.M. He was less certain of the noise he heard coming from the church sanctuary.

Colten thought it wrong to ever lock the door of the church. This charitable notion was often rewarded by having one or more of the town drunks sleeping it off on the Grayson Community Church's thin carpet. But in the August heat most celebrators chose to bed down outdoors.

"Those steps aren't coming from a pathetic, inebriated soul," Paul whispered to himself. "Someone is being very cautious . . ."

Paul Colten was sleeping in his clothes. He pivoted into a sitting position, put on his shoes, then left the cot and headed for the gun belt which lay in the bottom drawer of his desk.

He was behind the desk when the door of the office opened. In the darkness he couldn't tell much about the figure that entered, except the intruder was carrying a gun and wearing a hood over his head.

Colten spoke in mock friendliness. "In need of prayer, friend?"

The reply came in a voice deep and artificial. "You may be the one in need of prayer. Don't referee no fight and don't let Chinese into the church. The church is for Americans."

Rage gripped Paul Colten. "Sammy Wong and his family are Americans. Americans who don't need to wear hoods—"

Red and orange flashed in the office. Colten hit the floor as he heard a bullet cut into the wall behind him. The hooded figure turned and ran.

Paul grabbed his gun belt from the bottom desk drawer and took off after the intruder. His adversary must be very nervous to have missed him at such close range.

Buzzing filled his ears as Preacher Paul entered the sanctuary, but he could still hear the front double doors of the church being pushed open. The doors slammed shut as Paul ran toward them, strapping his gun belt around his waist.

Before going outside, he stopped and briefly worked his right arm and hand. A bullet wound from a year ago seemed to have completely healed. Well, almost completely.

Gun in hand, he stepped outside. He didn't stay there long. Bullets from two different directions winged into the wood of the church. Colten darted back inside. He closed one of the double doors and used it as a shield. Glancing around the door, he thought he spotted some movement behind the one large tree that fronted the church from about twenty yards away.

The gunmen knew where he was. He needed to improve the odds. The preacher figured men afraid to show their faces were good targets for mockery. "It's a hot night, gents, why not take off your hoods? Guess you're too yellow. Probably hid behind your momma's skirts when you were kids."

"Shut your damn mouth, preacher! We're gonna give you the hell you preach about!"

The voice was different from the one the preacher had heard in his office, and he thought he recognized it. He looked around the door and saw a figure behind the tree. A dot of lightning scampered about in his hand. The figure was lighting a torch.

Paul silently employed words wrong for a preacher as his first shot harmlessly burrowed into the cottonwood. A bullet exploded against the door inches from Colten and a cloud of wood shards spiked against his face.

That shot didn't come from behind the cottonwood. There was another gunman, lying on the ground, about ten yards to the side of the tree.

"Hellfire, Reverent, I'm bringin' it right at you!" It was the voice Colten recognized. Paul looked around the door as a figure carrying a lighted torch ran directly at him.

"Stop!" the pastor yelled.

"You're gonna burn, Preacher!" Sparks streamed from the flames as the runner pointed the torch toward the church. Colten launched a red flame into the runner's chest. The hooded figure stumbled but continued to move toward the church. "Hell's comin' . . ."

Colten's next shot sprawled the runner onto his back. The torch continued to burn and send sparks into the air. Only a few of those sparks needed to collide with the dry wood of the church to make the threats of hellfire very real.

Rance Dehner and Stacey Hooper exploded out through the batwings of the Mule Kick Saloon and ran toward the gunshots. They immediately spotted a figure sprinting several yards in front of them.

"Looks like the sheriff," Rance said.

"He runs very fast," Stacey acknowledged. "The taxpayers of Grayson are well served."

Sheriff Cal Markham continued his fast pace as he bolted up Main Street. Arriving at the town's final boardwalk, he jumped off and while continuing to run, drew his gun and fired in the direction of the church. His shot came from too far away to cause any harm, but it seemed to quell the threat. A dark outline, barely silhouetted by the burning torch on the ground, turned and vanished into the blackness of night. Hoofbeats pounded the air as the lawman, Rance and Stacey neared their destination.

His gun holstered, Preacher Paul darted toward the burning torch. He stamped the fire out as his rescuers drew near. Colten spoke as he breathed heavily. “Thank you, Gents, I sure needed the help.”

Stacey Hooper looked upward, then looked at the preacher. “The heavenly hosts must have been busy with other matters, so your Employer dispatched less worthy beings to provide you with assistance.”

All four men guffawed at the gambler’s remark, but the merriment was short lived. Cal Markham crouched over the corpse lying beside the still smoldering torch. The lawman showed no surprise as he yanked the hood off the dead man.

“Boone Witter,” Markham said.

“Boone was the first person I met when I arrived in town last night,” Dehner explained, “he seemed to be a real troublemaker.”

Cal rose from his crouch. “Yeh, Witter was a troublemaker, but didn’t have him the brains of a fence post. This attack on Preacher Paul was planned by someone smarter. One troublemaker is gone but we still got lots of trouble in front of us.”

Chapter Ten

Bo Kendrick sipped his morning coffee. His headache didn't subside. Last night had been typical. He had drunk too much and slept too little. Bo looked at the window shade which was still pulled down. In two hours or so he would have to lift it and begin another day as proprietor of Kendrick's Gun Shop.

Bo laughed bitterly, causing hot coffee to dribble over his chin. He might as well leave the shade down for all the business he was getting since young whatshisname set up a gun shop six months or so back. Well, let customers go to the young jasper. He was getting fed up with their complaints about guns not getting fixed right.

The complainers were right, and Kendrick knew it. The booze gave him unsteady hands.

"To hell with all of 'em," he muttered.

Bo Kendrick was an angry, hateful man. He had been that way for 18 months, ever since his wife died. Staring at the yellow glow emanating from a kerosene lamp on the store's work bench he once again lived through that awful day.

"But Doc, what if I take her east to one of them fine hospitals, maybe they can . . ."

Doctor Fred Cranston shook his head. "She wouldn't survive the trip, Bo. And even if she did, there's nothing they could do for her."

"No-good damn doctor," Kendrick said to a flickering light. "I'm glad someone had the sense to kill—"

The door to the shop opened. A familiar person stepped inside. "Heard about last night at the church?"

Kendrick belched out a few profanities, then answered the question. "I was in the Mule Kick when the first shots got fired. I joined the barflies who watched from afar. This thing has gone too far. I ain't gonna stir up crazy jaspers no more. They were jus' supposed to scare the preacher, not shoot at him or start a fire."

"You weren't so shy back in the election."

"Sure! I wanted to stop the chinks from taking over the town. But I never shot at no one. Count me out! If Grayson wants to go to hell, let it."

As Bo spoke, he gestured upward forgetting about the mug of coffee in his hand. The liquid flew upward and then slapped the back of his own neck as it came down. The store owner unleashed a barrage of curses. Those would be the last words he spoke.

His companion slammed a pistol against the side of Kendrick's head. He then dragged the unconscious body out the back door of the store. The attacker did a quick check of the alley, confirming that the area was vacant, then laughed contentedly as he pulled a knife from his belt.

Chapter Eleven

Rance Dehner marveled at the composure of the man who sat in the office of the *Grayson Herald.* Mack Wong was totally calm. An unusual demeanor for a man who had just been extensively questioned by the sheriff regarding a murder investigation.

Mack's serenity appeared genuine. The other four people in the office were trying, without success, to match the boxer's sense of peace. Mandy Wilsey was sitting in an office chair smiling nervously at Mack who sat in an identical chair facing her. Scoop Wilsey was leaning against a desk, also facing Mack.

Rance Dehner and Stacey Hooper were both on their feet, a situation necessitated by the lack of chairs. Both men frequently glanced toward the front window of the newspaper office where a crowd had gathered and was peering inside. Not all of the faces were friendly. Rance noticed a fair number of Asians scattered among the onlookers. He figured most of them were visitors recently arrived in Grayson to attend the fight on Saturday.

Scoop opened the meeting on an apologetic note. "Mack, I know we originally set up this interview to discuss your boxing match with Bill Connors, but well, after Bo Kendrick was found dead this morning, his throat cut . . .”

“I understand,” Mack replied in a quiet voice. “And I will tell you the same thing I told the sheriff and his deputy. I know nothing of Mr. Bo Kendrick’s unfortunate death. I never met the man.”

“But you were awake very early this morning?” Mandy’s eyebrows came together in a quizzical manner.

“Yes. I saddled a horse my uncle has lent me and rode about a half mile out of town. The manager at the livery has told the sheriff I was at the livery at about sunup. I tied up the horse in a small grove of trees and ran for about one hour. Peter Thomas was with me and can serve as a witness if that becomes necessary.”

Scoop asked the obvious. “The morning run was part of your training for the fight?”

“Yes,” Mack replied. “Though I run for an hour on most mornings. I intend to maintain that routine even after Saturday. My fight with Bill Connors will be my last.”

Mack’s serene countenance cracked a little with an amused smile. He had shocked all four of his companions and enjoyed doing it.

Scoop Wilsey was both stunned and excited. Mack Wong had just handed him a . . . well . . . a real scoop! “Why are you leaving boxing,

Mack? Your career is going great. So far, you are undefeated."

The boxer nodded his head. "I have used the name of the Dragon to do good for society. Now, I will use my reputation to benefit my family."

"In what way?" Mandy asked.

"There are many successful businesses in San Francisco that are owned by Chinese. Most are run by families."

Mack stopped speaking for a moment as if deciding how to explain his next point. Dehner decided to help him out. "And most of these successful businesses are in Chinatown. The owners are being harassed by tong gangs to pay protection money."

Mack smiled again, but there was sadness in it. "Tong gangs are a terrible threat in Chinatown. I will help the Chinese businesspeople deal with them."

"I have spent some time plying my trade in San Francisco," Stacey declared. "And found the police department there to be extraordinarily competent. A bit too much so, at times. Can't the local gendarmes provide assistance?"

The reply was polite but firm. "No. The police department is excellent in dealing with most crimes, but Chinatown is different. Very few officers speak Chinese or understand the culture. I plan to form a small but effective private force."

Dehner continued in a questioning manner. "I

suspect some businesses are also pressured to be fronts for opium dens?"

"Yes. There are many problems to deal with."

Stacey glanced at the crowd gawking from outside. "You will be a formidable adversary for the tong gangs, Mack. Is it possible a few of them have come to Grayson to, shall we say, ensure your plans to help your uncle are never realized?"

The boxer shook his head. "No. The tong gangs are vicious, but in a strange way, limited. They rarely operate outside of Chinatown. Many members of the gangs are young men who are illiterate . . . in any language. They stay in their cocoon."

Dehner began to pace about the office. "Let's talk about Bruiser Bill Connors. I did some research on him before coming to Grayson, and much of what your uncle has told me has confirmed my research. Connors has been boxing professionally since he was seventeen. He is now thirty-eight years old."

"That is old for a boxer," Mack said. "I am twenty-two. I believe it foolish for a man to box beyond the age of twenty-five."

Mack's response left Dehner surprised. In their past encounters the young man had only spoken in response to a question. Now, he had volunteered information.

The detective glanced at both Wilseys. They had also picked up on the change and would not resent Dehner taking over at least part of the interview. Mandy was taking notes.

Dehner continued: "Connors isn't undefeated, but he has had a great career in the ring."

"I saw him fight eighteen months ago in Denver," Mack again spoke up. "He was powerful. But all the punishment his body had endured has reduced some of that power. Mr. Connors had to move in closer than he once did to his opponent, Kid Hansen, to give his blows their full force. He won by using what is called, 'the oldest trick in the book.' "

"I'm always interested in how a man defeats an opponent with a trick," Stacey beamed.

"In the ninth round, Bill Connors began to stumble a bit and act woozy," Mack explained. "Kid Hansen, thinking Mr. Connors defeated, moved in very close for the kill. Mr. Connors knocked him out."

Mack Wong studied his hands for a moment. When he looked up his face reflected a winsome humor. "I saw him leaving the auditorium that night. Bruiser Bill Connors liked to be surrounded by admirers. You were there, Mr. Stacey, along with others, telling Bruiser Bill how magnificent he was. And the women, of course. Mr. Connors always wanted pretty women around him."

"All that has disappeared," Rance once again began to pace. "Reputation is often a step behind reality. Connors is now travelling from one small town to another, fighting locals and making what money he can from it. His promoter, Roscoe Platt, is all that remains of his circle of so-called friends."

A look of distaste now clouded Wong's face. "When my uncle contacted me about fighting Bruiser Bill I only saw an opportunity to help build the medical clinic. I now fear I might have put Bill Connors in an impossible situation."

"Bill Connors can't back down," Mandy gestured with her pencil as she spoke. "A reputation which took him twenty-one years to build would crumble overnight."

Dehner tugged on his ear. "There is another matter to consider. None of Connors' recent fights, including this one, has any official standing. That means there's no boxing commission to demand medical check-ups."

Scoop inhaled and ran a hand over his head. "Connors may be risking his life in the fight this Saturday."

"Perhaps," Mack acknowledged. "Bill Connors is an old, powerful bear who is cornered. A cornered bear is very dangerous."

Chapter Twelve

Bruiser Bill Connors stood on the boardwalk in front of Sammy's Hotel and Restaurant and smiled at the large crowd that was gathering. The smile was genuine. Grayson wasn't New York, Chicago or Denver but it was big enough and Bill Connors gained a special energy and joy from crowds.

He had noticed the hotel filling up with guests from outside Grayson. And that Scoop fella had told him newspapers all over the country were going to carry his write-up of the fight.

Yes, Bill Connors was big news again. And maybe, if he could knock out the chink, he'd stay big news.

Roscoe Platt stood beside his client, but his eyes were on the crowd. "Talk to 'em for a few minutes, Champ," he whispered. "We'll get a few more suckers here before we begin the autographs."

Roscoe had managed Bill Connors since the boxer's first professional fight. And after all these years, Connors still felt anger over Roscoe calling people who bought tickets and bought autographs as "suckers." But Bruiser Bill had long ago accepted the fact that his manager regarded everyone as lambs to be fleeced.

Connors noticed that Buck, the old deputy with a gimp, was standing near the back of the crowd. He was probably there in his official capacity. Bruiser Bill felt an instant bond with the deputy. Buck, like him, probably had to listen to a lot of fools telling him he was too old for his job.

Bruiser Bill held up one hand, waving it to quiet the crowd. "I wanna thank all of ya for comin' out. Ya see, this fella who calls himself 'the Dragon' has some perty strange ideas 'bout boxin'. He talks a lot 'bout modern boxin'. The Dragon thinks boxin' is sorta' like dancin'. I'm gonna knock that notion outta his head this Saturday!"

Loud cheers and prolonged laughter blasted forth from the crowd. The atmosphere became so raucous, no one at first noticed the tall, wiry, red-faced man at the rear who began shouting, "Kill the Dragon, Kill the dragon!"

Buck did notice. "Calm down, Jeff!"

Jeff Taggert ignored the deputy's command. He plowed through the mob, making his way to Bill Connors while continuing to shout, "Kill the Dragon" in a playful, childish voice.

Doctor Edward Ackerman was in the crowd; he approached Taggert and grabbed him by the arm. "Take it easy—"

"I ain't takin' orders from nobody." He pushed the doctor to the ground and the mood of the crowd changed. Some women screamed and shouts of "stop him!" erupted from the men.

Buck reached Jeff as he put a foot on the first of four steps leading to the boardwalk in front of the hotel. The deputy figured all that could be said to the troublemaker had been said. Buck clenched his hands into fists and pummeled Taggert's head.

Cheers emanated from the crowd once again as Jeff staggered sideways in an attempt to stay on his feet. Five yards away from the crowd, his attempt ended in failure. Taggert dropped to the ground.

"Sure glad I don't have ta fight Buck this Saturday!" Connors shouted.

Laughter and good cheer once again dominated the crowd. They began to center their attention on Roscoe, who began explaining the once in a lifetime opportunity that was only minutes away. "Bruiser Bill Connors will sign an autograph for the lowly price of . . ."

Both Buck and Doc Ackerman crouched over Jeff Taggert. They were on opposite sides of the unconscious man and had to move their heads close together to be heard above the excited crowd. "I don't think Jeff's drunk, Doc, if you ask me—"

"Jeff's been drinking laudanum," Ackerman cut in. "He tried to get some from me yesterday, made up some crazy sickness and demanded I give him the stuff. I refused. Later that day, Tom Bascomb told me two bottles of laudanum were missing from his store. Bascomb's Emporium is a big place. Tom is often there by himself and too busy—"

Buck's turn to interrupt: "I know that laudanum stuff can be good medicine sometimes, but it can sure drive a man crazy when not used proper-like. I don't think it should be sold in stores like rock candy."

"Tom Bascomb agrees with you," the doctor explained. "He's not going to order any more. He says most of the stuff gets stolen anyway. You know, there's serious talk in the East of taking drugs like laudanum out of the stores and making them only available to hospitals and doctors. That makes good sense to me."

A low moaning sound came from near the ground. Taggert was regaining consciousness. As he began to sit up, Jeb Smith, the head bartender at the Mule Kick, broke away from the crowd and joined the deputy and the doctor. "Can I help any?"

Ackerman looked at the bruises and swelling on Jeff's face. "Could you help me get this jasper back to my office? He needs to be patched up a bit."

Buck did a quick glance backward at the crowd now lining up for an autograph. "I'd be obliged to you, Jeb. I should stay here. This bunch sure is antsy."

"Sure. I feel sorry for Taggert, even though I've

had to throw him out of the Mule Kick plenty o' times."

"You probably won't have to do that much longer," Ackerman said.

Both of the doctor's companions looked surprised. Buck spoke for both of them. "Whaddya mean?"

Ackerman inhaled deeply and shook his head. "Laudanum drinkers don't last long."

Chapter Thirteen

Jenny Wong carried a tray of dirty dishes into the restaurant's kitchen and placed them on a counter. She ran a hand across her forehead wiping away perspiration. Around her, two people were scurrying about and talking to each other in Chinese.

The upcoming boxing match between the Dragon and Bruiser Bill Connors had brought a large number of visitors to Grayson and packed out Sammy's Hotel and Restaurant. The dinner hour had been very profitable and very hectic.

A noticeable number of the customers that night were Asians. Jenny leaned against a doorframe and giggled as she remembered her father's quip: "Americans think Asians very polite because we use word, 'honorable,' a lot."

Jenny had laughed at her father's remark. Her Auntie Wai Lan hadn't even smiled. But Auntie Wai Lan had dined at the restaurant that night, and perhaps learned an important lesson.

"Not all Asians are polite to people who serve them food," Jenny whispered to herself while giggling again.

The young woman began to speak in Chinese to the couple that served as cooks as she switched into her role of restaurant manager. There was little work left to do. A busy night was ending.

Despite all the hard work she had put in, Jenny Wong wasn't tired. On the contrary, she felt nervous and confused. Jenny had always been suspicious of the loony behavior associated with the word, "romance." In her mind, she classified as silly those girls who got all moony-eyed and ditsy over some cowboy.

But last night when she had seen Peter Thomas for the first time, she felt limp. And now the subject of her obsession was sitting in the dining area, sipping a sarsaparilla, and talking with Harold Cogan, the banker, and his wife Sylvia.

Harold and Sylvia often dined late. The banker's duties kept him chained to his desk long after the bank closed. Peter Thomas, who was waiting for Jenny, had struck up what seemed to the young woman to be a rather intense conversation with Mr. and Mrs. Cogan.

Jenny gave final instructions to her two person crew, quickly patted her hair, and then went out to meet Peter. But her first words were to the Cogans. "I hope Mr. Thomas has not bored you too much."

Jenny's eyes darted to Peter. Did he understand she was joking? He seemed to. Peter laughed along with Harold and Sylvia. Harold and Sylvia mumbled some polite words, then departed, obviously aware that their continued presence would hinder the two young folks.

Peter and Jenny casually strolled from the restaurant into the hotel lobby and then outside for their prearranged walk. Jenny Wong, who rarely took much interest in celestial matters, noted that this night was a big improvement over the previous one. A bright moon surrounded by a scattering of stars looked . . . well . . . very nice.

"You've had a pretty crazy night," Peter said.

The lady nodded her head. "The craziness started this afternoon. There was a fight of some kind before Mr. Connors sold autographs in the hotel lobby. The signing went on for at least two hours and . . ." the woman stopped speaking, then gave her companion a curious look. "What were you talking about with the Cogans?"

Peter's eyebrows shot up. "I was jawing with the Cogans about something that just might be very important to both of us."

"Oh."

"I told you about how I spent time in the army . . . a lot of it was spent rounding up horses and breaking them. The army doesn't like to do it. That's not what Uncle Sam builds forts out West for. But they still gotta do it. The army needs horses and often there's no place to buy 'em."

"Yes?" Jenny sounded confused.

Excitement filled Peter Thomas' voice. "The fort about fifteen miles from here is expanding; they'll need horses!"

Peter's exuberance baffled the young woman even more. "Yes, that is probably true."

"I plan to start Grayson's first horse ranch!" Peter declared.

Jenny allowed the young man's remark to bounce across her mind. She recalled with both alarm and excitement his opening statement about the dual importance of the news. She tried to keep a neutral voice. "Grayson's banker seems to believe your plan is sound, which is certainly a good sign. I wish you well in your endeavor, Peter." Jenny paused, thinking it wise perhaps to leave it there. No. She needed to know what he was thinking.

"Peter, you said your news was important to both of us. I must confess to being confused. What did you mean?"

Peter Thomas shrugged his shoulders in an exaggerated manner and gave his companion a comical smile. "Well, if I want to start a horse ranch near Grayson, that means I gotta leave San Francisco and move here. Doesn't that just make you plumb delirious with happiness, Jenny Wong?"

Jenny turned her face away as she laughed. Yes, the news made her very happy, but she wasn't about to confess it openly. "Peter, I will—"

The couple were caught up in the joy of a budding relationship. Neither paid attention to the world around them. They only knew that suddenly they were grabbed and hurled against their will into darkness. Peter stumbled, fell, and bent in pain as a hard boot slammed into his ribs. A hooded figure stood over him, and a deep voice threatened, "The Dragon better not fight, or the lady dies."

Peter rolled, then sprang back onto his feet. Instinctively, he lifted his arms into a boxer's position.

But this wasn't a match being held in his father's gymnasium. A blow to the back of his head blurred Peter's vision and collapsed his knees. As he dropped to the ground, he heard Jenny's muffled scream.

Buck sipped his own bad coffee, then looked at the two men who had been pestering him for every bit of information he had regarding the upcoming fight and just about everything else that had been going on in town. It was time for them to answer some questions. "The way I see it, this Roscoe Platt fella is one conniving rascal. Ya think maybe he's the one behind them strange messages Sammy Wong got?"

Stacey Hooper casually waved his hand as if brushing away the question. "No. The messages arrived before Roscoe's dismal debut in Grayson. He would have needed to employ assistants. Roscoe's skullduggery is a one man operation."

Rance Dehner smiled inwardly at the expression on Buck's face. The deputy appeared both flabbergasted and fascinated by Stacey's speech.

Rance and Stacey were in the sheriff's office going over information with Buck. Cal Markham was doing a round.

Dehner tugged on his right ear. "Before all the hoorawing began over the boxing match, was there any trouble in Grayson between the Wongs and anyone else?"

Buck tilted his head as if literally running the question over his mind. "Well, sorta. Some fools sounded off durin' the race fer mayor. But that didn't amount to all that much. I guess folks who had a bug in their ear 'bout Sammy and his family kept their notions to themselves. Not till—"

The office door banged open and a boy of about nine ran in. Buck immediately spotted the serious look on the boy's face. "Hello, Roger." The deputy turned to his companions and pointed at the newcomer. "This is Roger Bascomb, his pa runs Bascomb's Emporium."

The boy spoke quickly, running his words together. "Pa sent me over to the newspaper with stuff for his advertisement." He held up a piece of paper, shook it, then continued. "Sheriff Markham stopped me and tole me ta come get ya. There's trouble somewhere between the newspaper place and the Mule Kick."

"Thanks Roger, now git back to your pa."

Roger obeyed the deputy's instructions as Buck, Stacey and Dehner ran in the direction of the Mule Kick. Once they had passed the *Grayson Herald*, another set of footsteps began pounding behind them. Dehner turned his head quickly. Scoop Wilsey was tailing them. No surprise.

Patches of yellow glow streamed from the windows of the businesses along the boardwalk. Four horsemen could be spotted in the middle of the street. At least two of them were holding guns. One of them fired into the shadow of an alley. A sharp sound of gunfire exploded from the darkness.

"We ain't close enough ta make our guns mean anything," Buck puffed out his words. He moved remarkably fast; somehow his bad leg didn't slow him down.

The horsemen turned their steeds and began to ride out of town. A figure sprang from the alley and shot at the escaping outlaws. One of the gang returned fire. The bullet ricocheted off a rock with a shrill scream and hit the side of Sheriff Cal Markham's leg.

The lawman folded and dropped to the ground as hoofbeats pounded out of the town. Dehner thought he heard a strange, frantic whine accompanying the retreating horses.

Cal Markham was struggling to get to his feet as the four men reached him. "I gotta get after those jaspers."

“Take it easy, Cal,” Buck ordered. “Your leg’s bleedin’ bad. You need the doc.”

Markham dropped back to the ground. “They’ve got Jenny Wong!”

Before any of the four men could reply, Cal pointed down the alley. “Thomas, the young Thomas, is back there unconscious.”

“We need to get movin’.” Buck’s face and voice were grim. “Scoop, you take care of matters here. The rest of us need to git back to the office. Our horses there are fresh. We got a hard ride ahead of us.”

Chapter Fourteen

Buck dismounted and examined the trail. "When ya track at night, ya can't jus' study on it. Ya gotta use your imagination a spell and try to think like the owlhoots."

Rance and Stacey remained on their horses, hoping Buck's imagination wasn't hitting empty chambers. They were about three quarters of a mile outside of Grayson. The road was becoming more rock infested. The mountains made jagged silhouettes against the bright moon.

Buck began to speak in a monotone, more to himself than to his companions. "Skeet Carson was a fine man, we us'ta play checkers. He came out here from Ohia, wanted to git away from his factory job and start a ranch."

The deputy paused, gazed around him, then continued. "Everthin' went wrong for Skeet. He had ta pack up his family and head back ta Ohia. Hope that factory job ain't eatin' at him."

Buck's voice gained force. "I think those kidnappers are takin' Jenny to the old Carson ranch. The whole town knows 'bout it bein' abandoned and, from what I see, the trail is headin' that way."

Dehner placed both hands on the horn of his saddle and leaned toward the lawman. "But, since everyone knows about the Carson ranch, would the outlaws go there?"

"Jenny Wong is one very perty lady." Buck mounted his strawberry roan as he continued to speak. "We're dealin' with rats. Rats don't think with their brains. They're controlled by another part of the body. The way I see it, those thugs plan to pleasure themselves with Jenny tonight, then head for a hideout at sunup."

Buck spurred his horse as he turned it right. Dehner and Hooper followed.

The three men slowed their horses as they approached a knoll that fronted the Carson ranch. They ground tethered the steeds, then cautiously made their way up the small hill. Arriving at the top, they lay flat down on the earth.

From a first glance, Dehner thought to himself that Skeet Carson had chosen a good location to fulfill his dream. Behind the ranch was a green forested area indicating water was nearby. Green appeared to frame the ranch, providing plenty of grass for hungry cows. The ranch house was a small but sturdy structure. Small and sturdy could also describe the barn to the left of the house.

Stacey Hooper's initial observation hit on the negative. "I don't mean to call into question your judgment, Buck, but I don't see any horses . . ."

"There's a corral in the back. That's where they got the horses." The lawman handed the telescope he had been using to Stacey. "Look careful at the side window on the left, Mr. Fancy Pants, you'll see yella light. There's at least two lanterns on in there, one of 'em seems to be movin'."

"Indeed," the gambler replied cheerfully as he utilized the telescope. "I apologize for questioning your judgment."

"Don't really mind the judgment stuff, it's that poker game last night that's still prodding me," Buck confessed. "Ya sure ya wasn't cheatin' maybe jus' a mite?"

"Buck, you have my assurances as a gentleman . . ."

Rance Dehner shushed his friend and pointed to the ranch house where a figure carrying a lantern stepped out of the front door and headed toward the barn. He was wearing a black hood.

Dehner's whisper was caustic. "Jenny's captors are local citizens of Grayson. They figure she might recognize them."

"What d' ya think he's goin' to the barn fer?" the deputy asked.

"Don't know," Dehner replied. "Let's pay him a visit and find out."

The three men quickly descended the knoll. Dehner dropped to one knee and peeked around the small hill. "The hooded jasper is entering the barn; now's the time for our social call."

Dehner and his two companions ran to the barn and flattened themselves against the front. The barn's overhang shrouded them in a deep darkness making it unlikely they would be spotted by the other three outlaws in the ranch house.

Rance drew his gun and advanced toward the open double doors. Buck and Stacey followed immediately behind him. The glow coming out of the barn was steady. Their prey had hung the lantern and was now going about his business.

Rance glanced inside the building. The hooded figure was carrying a large bale of straw towards him. The man was almost at the door. Dehner rushed inside. The outlaw dropped the straw and started to go for his gun. Dehner slammed his Colt against the thug's face.

"Stay quiet or I'll kill you!" Dehner whispered to the fallen outlaw as he crouched over him and yanked the hood off his head.

The face was young and pale. Blood smeared one side, which was already beginning to swell from Dehner's assault.

The detective looked up at Buck. "Recognize him?"

Buck nodded his head. "Seen him 'round town. Don't know who he is."

"What's your name?" Rance demanded. "And keep your voice low."

"Arnie."

The detective asked a question for which he already knew the answer. "What were you getting the straw for?"

Absolute evil filled the outlaw's eyes. "Ain't no bed or nothin' in the house. We wanted somethin' soft like on the floor to have ourselfs some fun with the chink girlie."

There was nothing apologetic or even uneasy in the man's voice. Arnie felt no remorse for what he and his accomplices were planning.

Dehner felt revulsion toward his captive, but this was not the time to express it. "Who's your boss man, Arnie?"

Terror flooded over the young man's face, washing away everything else. "Ain't saying."

"We'll deal with this later," Dehner spoke anxiously as he yanked the gun from Arnie's holster and tossed it onto a rotting pile of straw. "Stacey, I want you to change clothes with Arnie."

"What a perfectly dreadful request!" The gambler's whisper resounded with genuine alarm. "Even the briefest sniff taken from a distance reveals that Arnie hasn't bathed in months. Those filthy clothes must contain the dust and dirt of the ages, to say nothing of the crawling inhabitants of the garments!"

"Arnie is exactly your size," Dehner pleaded. "We need to get inside the ranch house and . . ."

"I'm sorry, good friend, I've ridden some hard trails with you, but a line must be drawn somewhere." Stacey declared piously.

"Ya limeys think you're better than the rest of us," Buck snapped. "Let me tell ya—"

“Quiet, both of you,” Dehner demanded. “I’ll put on Arnie’s clothes, then we’ll tie him up and gag him. There’s not much light in the ranch house and I’ll be carrying the bale. They probably won’t notice the difference in our size. After I get inside, I’ll stall them for a couple of minutes. I want you two to get to the ranch house windows and get ready to back me up.”

“Back ya up as ya do what?” Buck asked.

“I haven’t worked that part out yet.”

Dehner’s thoughts were grim as he entered the ranch house carrying the bale of straw and a lantern. The hood over his head was blood stained on one side. He was hoping that in the darkness, the three remaining kidnappers wouldn’t notice.

Lewd laughter and mindless profanity filled what had once been a living room. A stone fireplace stood in the middle of the large room containing a cold scattering of ashes.

Buck had been right. The outlaws had located two lanterns in the deserted house. The one lantern that had remained in the house gave out a light from where it stood in a corner. Rance could see the terror in Jenny’s face. She was lying on the floor, her hands and feet tied and her mouth gagged. The young woman’s blouse had been ripped.

“Arnie’s here with the straw, sweetie! Now we

can get down to some serious pleasure," one of the three hooded figures shouted.

"Git down, is a good way of puttin' it!"

Laughter again exploded in the room. The outlaw who had announced Arnie's arrival now shouted, "Don't stand there, fool, get over here with the straw."

Dehner put his light down and followed instructions. As the three hooded figures began to pick apart the bale and make a bed of the straw, the outlaw who had spoken first shouted again, "Bring that damn lantern over here, Arnie, we don't wanna miss out on any of the great scenery."

Dehner began to follow orders. As he picked up the lantern, he did a quick scan of the windows located on each side of the front door. Buck was at the nearest one and Stacey at the other. A large window ran across the back wall of the ranch house and Dehner wished one of his accomplices stood there. But the situation presented no opportunity to reorganize.

"We got ourselfs a right nice bed here," the voice came from the outlaw who previously hadn't spoken. "Let's put Snow White on it."

"Didn't know Snow White was a chink," replied the thug who had been giving instructions.

The three kidnappers indulged themselves in laughter for the last time. Rance set down the lantern and palmed his Colt. "Put your hands high, gents. All three of you!"

Harsh, confused voices yelled almost in unison.

"What the hell's gotten into you, Arnie?"

"That ain't Arnie—"

An explosion of glass was followed by the ring of a bullet as it ricocheted off the fireplace. Gunfire sounded from outside, but Dehner hadn't time to wonder why. All four men in the room hit the floor. Three of them knew there was an enemy in their midst and drew their guns, preparing to fire at the intruder posing as Arnie.

Dehner threw the lantern across the room, not wanting to be laying in a spotlight for the gunmen. The room became darker as a crashing sound came from a side wall. Only an unsteady yellow glow emanating from the far corner provided light.

Dehner spotted one man as he rolled away from the detective and drew his gun. Dehner's shot burrowed into the man's forehead. An attempt at a scream cut through Jenny's gag. Rance looked at the girl for a moment, not seeing the shadow which rose onto one knee to get a better shot at the detective.

Buck saw it. He fired from the window. The shadow gave a very unmuffled screech and dropped to the floor.

"Do you see the other one, Buck?" Dehner yelled.

"No, I—"

Breaking glass exploded from the back of the

house, followed by sounds of a man trying a desperate escape. “Look after Jenny,” Rance yelled at Buck as he pointed at the girl, then darted toward the back of the house.

He jumped through the broken window as a horse bolted from the corral behind the ranch house and galloped toward a trail which led into the woods. Dehner looked at the four remaining horses in the corral. They were all saddled.

Running past the recently opened gate in the corral, Rance gave a quick pat on the neck to the first horse whose reins he could grab. All the horses were tired, their needs ignored by the kidnappers who had their own desires in mind.

Dehner mounted the buckskin and guided it out of the corral. He kneed the horse toward a vanishing dust cloud at the start of a trail that cut into a forested area. He prodded the animal into a modest run. His adversary seemed to be panicking and spurring his horse into a speed impossible to maintain for a tired animal. A slower pace meant a more reliable mount.

Entering the trail, Rance could hear hoofbeats from not too far up ahead. Several yards away, the trail veered, and his adversary was now out of sight. But the detective’s initial assessment seemed to be correct. The still invisible animal was slowing its pace.

Dehner also slowed the pace of his buckskin. The hoofbeats coming from the fleeing outlaw suddenly stopped. His adversary could be waiting for him in ambush. Rance dismounted, ground tethered the buckskin, and drew his gun.

He cautiously approached the turn in the trail. Overhanging tree branches provided the cover of darkness as he stepped around the turn and faced what lay ahead.

Confusion was the detective's first response. About ten yards in front of him a horse was nibbling on leaves. Dehner couldn't see the ground surrounding the horse clearly. A lot of bullets had been flying only a few minutes ago. The escaping outlaw could have been wounded and fallen off his horse.

Then again . . .

Dehner moved toward the horse making as little noise as possible. As he neared the animal, he could see that the ground nearby contained no human bodies. Maybe the outlaw was hiding somewhere . . .

Rance Dehner's face crunched up as he silently cursed himself. He kept his gun drawn, almost hoping at this point to be walking into an ambush.

Nothing happened. Dehner mounted the chestnut and began the ride back to the corral. He spurred the horse a little too hard, then patted the animal in an apologetic manner. "It's not your fault that I fell for one of the oldest tricks in the book."

The escaping kidnapper had opened the corral gate and given the chestnut a hard swat.

The animal had responded by galloping off on the nearby trail. “The snake didn’t even have to hide all that carefully,” Rance whispered angrily to himself. “I didn’t look around at all. I just grabbed the buckskin and took off after a riderless horse.”

Dehner halted the chestnut and picked up the reins of the buckskin who was still tethered where he had left it. “I know this much, there is now one less horse in that corral. After I left, the kidnapper left in another direction. He’s headed back to town and his ruse as a respectable citizen.”

Rance sighed deeply as he arrived at the corral and found his suspicion about one less horse to be true. The detective suddenly realized he was still wearing a hood. He snatched it off. “I hope I get another chance to meet up with this respectable citizen . . . real soon.”

Chapter Fifteen

Rance took care of the horses, then hurried to the front of the ranch house, where he saw no one but heard activity coming from the barn. He made a fast run to the barn. Inside, the scene was busy but calm. Buck was harnessing two horses to a rickety buckboard. Dehner recognized the steeds as the ones he and Stacey had been riding.

As Rance drew nearer, the scene began to take on a somber tone. Jenny and Stacey were on the flatbed of the wagon, tending to Arnie who appeared to be unconscious.

"I have stopped the bleeding," Jenny was saying. "That is all I can do. We need to get him to Doctor Ackerman as soon as possible."

Stacey began to reply but stopped when he saw Rance approaching. "Welcome back, good friend, I note with regret that you have returned without a prisoner."

Dehner quickly explained how he had been fooled. While doing so, he focused most of his attention on Jenny Wong. The young woman was completely composed, on the outside anyway. In the light provided by the surviving lantern, he could see bruises on her arms and wrists. Otherwise, she appeared unhurt. Somewhere, Jenny had found a pin or some instrument to hold her ripped blouse together.

Jenny Wong spoke immediately after Rance had finished his explanation, closing the opportunity for Stacey and Buck to indulge in mockery. "Mr. Dehner, I have already thanked Mr. Hooper and Deputy Buck for helping me. I wish to also thank you. I will forever be grateful to you three men."

While assuring the lady she owed nothing to the threesome that rescued her, Dehner noticed the different reactions to Jenny's gratitude. Stacey beamed, almost looking like he was about to take a bow. Buck looked away, pretending to check the harnesses on the horses. Rance couldn't be sure, but he thought the deputy's face was red.

Dehner wondered casually if there had ever been any woman in Buck's life. Men outnumbered women in the West and Rance guessed Buck had a shyness which had kept him isolated from female attentions.

Stacey nodded at the unconscious body on the flatbed, which was naked from the waist up. "I tied this villain after you took his clothes for the charade. He was robed only in his unmentionables. When he broke his bonds, the no-good located your trousers and put them on before creating mischief. We must give the chap credit. He did observe a certain degree of propriety."

Rance had no interest in Arnie's observance of propriety. "How exactly did he get free?"

Hooper shook his head as if mourning the sad

state of a fallen world. "Alas, the rope was old and, no doubt, of poor quality. He must have broken the wretched thing—"

"That ain't true!" Buck shouted angrily as he stooped over, picked up the rope and pointed at the large knots which were still there. "Ya were sa proud of these knots, ya didn't make it tight enough. Arnie slipped his hands right through!"

Stacey shrugged his shoulders. "Perhaps—"

Buck wasn't finished. "And ya left his gun lyin' 'round. Damn near got me killed."

Embarrassment suddenly covered the deputy's face once again. "Ah, pardon me, ma'am, sorry 'bout the cussin'."

Jenny pressed her lips together to suppress a laugh before replying. "There is no need to apologize, Deputy Buck. Your language is always colorful and a delight to hear."

Buck looked at the ground and mumbled something. Rance changed the mood with a pragmatic question. "What happened after Arnie got ahold of my trousers and his gun?"

"He snuck outta the barn and got as close to me as he could," Buck answered. "He shot at me and missed by an inch or so. The bullet went through the winda."

Stacey spoke up, lifting an index finger in the air. "I immediately moved to correct my earlier oversight. I fired two bullets into Arnie, relegating him to his current helpless state."

Dehner nodded his head. "What about the outlaws in the house?"

"Both barflies, both dead," Buck immediately replied. "One of 'em called hisself, 'Wyoming,' meanin' he probably never got in spittin' distance of Wyoming. Don't know the name of the other jasper, seen 'im 'round some."

This time, Buck began to inspect the harnesses in earnest. "I'll git a couple men in the mornin'. We'll come back and bury what'll be left of them owlhoots after the coyotes have their feast. No time now, gotta git Arnie to Doc Ackerman. Arnie knows the name of the boss man."

Stacey's voice had entirely regained its usual cheerful tone. "When Arnie learns that cooperation with the law will keep him from a noose, I suspect he will choose the path of good citizenship, if somewhat belatedly."

Rance pointed backward with his thumb. "We'll be needing two horses. I'll fetch them from the corral."

"I will accompany you." Jenny hopped off the wagon and joined the detective.

Rance was surprised. The young woman was always unfailingly polite. To simply announce that she was tagging along was totally out of character.

They were only a short distance out of the barn when Dehner understood Jenny's forwardness.

"Mr. Dehner, I need to hear the truth from

you," the lady's voice was melodic but pleading. "Mr. Hooper and Deputy Buck have assured me that Mr. Peter Thomas was not seriously injured in the attack. But I fear they may be softening the truth to spare my feelings."

"None of us saw Peter," Rance said honestly. "But we left Scoop Wilsey in charge and I'm sure he got Peter to the doctor immediately. And I'm also pretty sure that right now, Peter Thomas is gazing out a window every two minutes to see if you are coming back. You're the best medicine he could have, so let's get that medicine to him as quick as we can."

They ran the rest of the way to the corral.

Chapter Sixteen

The deputy drove the buckboard with Jenny on the flatbed tending as best she could to Arnie. Rance and Stacey were on horses. Their arrival in Grayson seemed to set off chaos.

The buckboard stopped at Doctor Ackerman's house, where Jenny ran inside. She learned Peter Thomas had suffered a minor concussion and had returned to Sammy's Hotel and Restaurant. As she bolted from the house she was greeted by Peter and her family, all of whom had been watching for her safe return. Sammy led the happy group back to the establishment which bore his name.

Peter Thomas, his father, and the Wong family were not the only ones keeping watch. Grayson's two journalists, Scoop and Mandy Wilsey, both walked into the doctor's house moments after Jenny departed. Clyde anxiously stood beside the couple as the deputy inquired after his boss.

"How's Cal, Doc?" Buck asked as he reached down and scratched the dog's ears.

"Not bad," the doctor answered. "The bullet passed through the side of his leg. It must have skimmed the artery, 'cause he lost an awful lot of blood. He'll be okay, though. He's back at his office drinking a lot of water, if he has any sense."

"Looks like fer a while I won't be the only lawdog 'round here who limps!" Buck chuckled. He gave Clyde a pat on the head, then left to check on his boss.

Ackerman grimaced at Clyde but decided not to make an issue of the dog. "I will need some help operating on this man, Mandy." The doctor pointed to Arnie, who now lay on a table in the surgery.

"I will do everything I can, Doctor."

There was nothing Scoop, Stacey or Rance could do. All three men left the doctor's house and noted that Grayson was still a very busy place despite the late hour.

"News must be getting around about Jenny's rescue," Scoop commented. "There seems to be a party going on."

Stacey pulled a cigarillo from the front pocket of his coat. "We are entering those wee hours where men feel invincible and very confident when it comes to challenging the odds. I'm on my way to the Mule Kick to take bets on Saturday's fight."

As Stacey hurried off, Rance continued to walk with Scoop. They were apparently going to the sheriff's office, but Dehner didn't really care.

On the ride back from the Carson place the detective had been trying to find a pattern in the tragedies which had devastated Grayson. He was beginning to find some connection, however vague, between the various acts of violence and death.

Scoop didn't notice his friend's distraction. He was chuckling over Doctor Ackerman's obvious disapproval of Clyde. "Clyde's been beside Mandy from the first time she helped Doc Cranston with an operation. Cranston didn't mind at all, but Ackerman . . ."

"Doc Cranston was a fine man," Dehner cut in. "He was alert to everything going on around him. He even helped me trap a killer."

"He sure did. I remember that well."

"Do you think there could be a tie-in between Doctor Cranston's murder, the killing of Bo Kendrick, and all the violence over the boxing match?"

Scoop looked surprised, then confused. "Well . . . maybe . . ."

"I wonder if Bascomb's Emporium is open?" Dehner asked.

Scoop's confusion increased. "Bascomb's usually closes a lot earlier than this. But, what with all the visitors in town and the excitement over Jenny being rescued, not to mention the boxing match, it might be worth Tom's while to stay open."

"If we can, let's pay a visit to the store before we see the sheriff."

The store was open, and Tom Bascomb was pleased to chat. "People have been in here jawing about all the goings on. I know you two gents have been busy. Grab some gumdrops for yourselfs and take some to Buck and Sheriff Markham."

Buck received the candy joyfully, but the sheriff's mood was grim. "This town is acting like the circus is here. Which, in a way, I suppose it is. I gotta get outta this here office and—"

Dehner interrupted. "You need to stay off that leg and get a good night's sleep. Scoop and I can help Buck keep things in order."

The sheriff reluctantly agreed and left for home. Rance and Scoop initially remained in the office while Buck did a round. When the deputy returned, he gave a brief report, "Folks are actin' crazy, but not shootin' each other. Not yet, anyways."

Armed with that information, and temporarily wearing deputy badges, the detective and the reporter began to check out Grayson for themselves. Their first stop was the town's hub, the Mule Kick Saloon.

A tired looking but still amicable Jeb Smith was tending bar. "It might be sunup before these jaspers leave." He nodded in the direction of a distant table. "Your friend is doing swift business taking bets on the fight. The boss is also doing great business tonight. I hear he's even opened up the restaurant."

When the acting deputies arrived at Sammy's Hotel and Restaurant, they found that Jeb's report was wrong. The restaurant wasn't serving customers. Sammy had pushed several of the restaurant's tables together. The entire Wong family were sitting with Peter and Barry Thomas, talking over tea, coffee, and pie.

Everyone sitting at the tables smiled and greeted Dehner and Wilsey. But Dehner noted a sense of unease which seemed to envelope the group. He figured Jenny and Peter were the probable cause. They were sitting together holding hands.

Rance was a bit startled to see Mack Wong sitting with his family. "Mack, Scoop and I have pretty much covered this town. I haven't spotted Bill Connors anywhere. Your opponent is probably sleeping, getting ready for the fight. Shouldn't you be doing the same thing?"

Mack smiled and nodded his head once. "Jenny's abduction made it impossible for me to sleep because of worry. Her safe return makes me too happy to sleep."

"He's already allowing Bruiser Bill to call the shots on making it a bare knuckle battle, might as well give him an advantage in the sleep department too." Barry Thomas tried to make his remark sound like a joke but couldn't quite bring it off.

Mandy Wilsey entered the restaurant looking

pale but happy. The woman embraced her husband who she was surprised and happy to see, then proclaimed, "It looks like Arnie is going to make it. There's a chance he will tell us the person responsible for kidnapping Jenny . . . and probably, for a lot of other things too!"

"Is Arnie awake right now?" Scoop asked his wife.

"Yes," Mandy's voice became grim. "Doctor Ackerman thinks Arnie is a laudanum drinker. He's not responding to the dose the doctor gave him earlier in the usual manner. He's awake now and . . ."

The woman shook her head as if waking herself up. "Arnie is weak and the doctor sent me here to see that his patient gets a little food . . . soup maybe . . . before Arnie goes back to sleep."

"Of course!" Jenny declared and began to get up.

"Remain where you are, child!" Wai Lan, Jenny's aunt, spoke in a soft but commanding voice. "I will prepare soup and take it to the doctor's house."

Jenny remained half standing. "But I know the kitchen well . . ."

"You must allow your auntie opportunity to be useful." Wai Lan stood up and headed for the kitchen. The issue resolved; Jenny once again sat down beside Peter. She didn't appear too upset about it.

Mandy took a backward step. “I have to get to the church. Arnie is asking for a preacher.”

“Great!” Rance exclaimed. “If Arnie is worried about his soul, he isn’t too worried about harm from earthly powers. I’ll run to the church and get Preacher Paul.”

Mandy shook her head. “You’ve already done so much, Rance—”

Sammy Wong arose from his chair and smiled in a manner that was almost pleading. “Please, Mr. and Mrs. Wilsey, join us at our table. I would be honored to have the editor of the *Grayson Herald* and Grayson’s angel of mercy to have food and drink with me, my family and close friends.”

Dehner was surprised and more than a bit moved. Sammy Wong could be a gracious host, in the very best sense, when the occasion called for it. “You folks stay here,” he said to the Wilseys, “I’m going to church.”

Chapter Seventeen

Preacher Paul stood under the cottonwood tree that fronted the Grayson Community Church. That same tree had only the night before provided cover for gunslingers trying to kill him.

He was watching the bustle that raged in Grayson. The noise from the saloons sounded oddly pathetic at a distance; the laugher conveyed far more desperation than amusement.

Paul Colten needed at times to distance himself from the harshness of life in a frontier town. Eternal truths could get lost in the day to day brutality of survival. Besides, the bad news he needed to hear always found him soon enough.

The pastor spotted news of some kind trotting toward him. Was it . . . yes . . . it was Rance Dehner. Paul Colten left the isolation of the cottonwood and ran toward the detective, "What is it, Rance?"

Dehner delivered a quick summary of Jenny's kidnapping and rescue. "Arnie wants to talk with a preacher. He must be thinking about the afterlife. My thinking is more worldly. I'd like the name of the boss man who ordered the kidnapping."

Colten gave a crooked smile. "Maybe tonight we can address both heavenly and earthly needs."

The two men made quick time to Doctor Ackerman's house. As they entered his surgery, they saw Wai Lan carefully and slowly moving a spoonful of soup into Arnie's mouth.

Ackerman huddled with the preacher and the detective. "Our man is very weak. As you can see, Arnie's conscious, but he'll be sleeping soon and he needs the rest. You can't talk to him very long."

A weak, wavery whisper sounded in the room. "No more."

"Are you sure?" Wai Lan's voice was soft and comforting.

"Yes . . . no more . . ."

Wai Lan smiled at the three men standing in the room, bowed, and then left, soup and spoon in hand. Paul Colten took her place beside the wounded gunman.

"Arnie, people call me Preacher Paul, I'm the pastor of the church here in Grayson."

"Heard of ya. Ya us'ta be Reverend Colt . . . a gunfighter . . ."

"Yes."

"Did . . . did God forgive ya for the killings . . ."

"Yes. I know he did."

"I've done bad things . . . very bad . . . don't wanna go ta hell . . . can . . ." Arnie words became slurred and senseless. Then he fell into a sleep.

Paul Colten looked at Dehner. "Looks like I

wasn't much help to either heaven or earth."

Dehner grimaced as he spoke to the doctor. "How long do you think he'll sleep?"

"Hard to say," Ackerman replied. "Arnie may wake up in the night, but he probably won't be lucid."

Dehner couldn't leave it there. "When will we be able to talk with him?"

Ackerman flipped both hands in the air. "Who knows? My guess would be close to noon."

The former Reverend Colt pointed to one of the two empty beds in the surgery. "Mind if I sleep here tonight, doctor? I want to be around in case Arnie does wake up and feels like talking."

"You're a better man than me, Preacher. I don't care a thimble full of spit for Arnie's soul." This time Ackerman waved one hand in the direction of the empty beds. "Sure, make yourself comfortable."

"Thanks."

Dehner left the doctor's house and, functioning as an acting deputy, did a round of Grayson. Raucous shenanigans were still boiling up and spilling out of the saloons, but matters seemed to be under control. Bullets went into the air, not into bodies. His duty completed, Rance stopped in at Sammy's, where the gathering inside the restaurant was breaking up.

Dehner's bad news about Arnie falling into a deep sleep before he could give any information about his boss did create a somber mood. Jenny's aunt remained hopeful, "The gentleman ate a little less than half of the soup I brought him. I hope this sustain him through the night and he will be more talkative in the morning."

Wai Lan's statement did provide an upbeat note on which to end the evening. Rance quickly surveyed the Wongs and their guests. Barry Thomas looked worried and unhappy. But then, he always did. Peter Thomas and Jenny were in their own world.

The rest of the group were hard to peg except for Mandy and Scoop Wilsey. "I'll come back to the sheriff's office with you, Rance."

"You've done enough, Scoop. You and Mandy both need some sleep. Things are winding down. Buck and I can keep the lid on."

Rance walked out of Sammy's Hotel and Restaurant with the Wilseys, then stood outside on the boardwalk and watched them walk home together. As the night enveloped them, Scoop put an arm around his wife, and she rested her head on his shoulder.

An emptiness Dehner carried with him twisted at the core of his soul. He looked up at the sky, which looked back with indifference. He felt isolated and desperately alone.

Then, he remembered Sammy Wong was depending on him to find out who was threatening his nephew. The person or persons behind all the terror in Grayson were vicious and cared nothing for human life.

He whispered to himself, “Stop feeling sorry for yourself and get to work.”

Rance Dehner headed back to the sheriff’s office.

Chapter Eighteen

Mandy Wilsey opened her eyes and glanced at the bedroom window. Through the lace curtains she could tell the sky outside was a light gray.

Her husband lying beside her was still asleep. On most mornings, Scoop was the first to get out of bed. Mandy smiled as she reflected on the fact that when she served as a nurse, she always arose early to check on her patient.

The woman quietly left the bed and began to prepare for the day. She dressed, then went into the kitchen to fix some coffee. As she busied herself with that task her eyes became moist. She recalled that Doctor Cranston had, somehow, seen in her the ability to help him perform operations. The snake who had killed such a fine man needed to be brought to justice, soon.

The coffee made, Mandy poured herself a cup, leaned against the counter and continued to think back on what Doc Cranston had said, "A lot of women helped doctors attend to wounded soldiers during the war between the states. They learned nursing the hard way, just like you."

"Times change," the woman mused to herself. "Today, a woman can train to be a nurse at a school in the East. What if I had—"

Stirring sounds came from the bedroom. She

put her near-empty cup down on the counter and headed back to the bedroom, stopping at the open doorway. "Good morning, sleepy head."

"Good morning, beautiful." Scoop said that to Mandy every morning. She hadn't grown tired of it.

"I'm going to look in on Arnie. There's coffee made. Be back soon." Scoop replied by giving his wife a salute.

Outside, the sky had turned red. Mandy inhaled, and for a moment, took it all in.

She didn't want to be a nurse, not full time anyway. She loved her life in the West where she could be a part time nurse while working full time at the *Grayson Herald.* Not only that, every Sunday and Wednesday she played the piano and sometimes the guitar as she led the singing at Grayson Community Church.

The woman laughed softly and began to walk toward Doctor Ackerman's house. Yes, most of all, she enjoyed being married to Phineas, make that Scoop, Wilsey. "I'm very blessed," she said out loud.

The blessings continued when she arrived at Doctor Ackerman's house. Ackerman frequently locked his door at night but just as frequently he forgot. Last night had been one of the forgetful episodes.

Mandy walked in and headed directly for the surgery where she was surprised to see Paul

Colten putting on his shoes as he sat on one of the beds. “Good morning, Preacher.”

“Good morning.” Colten spotted the curious look on the woman’s face. “Ackerman said Arnie could wake up in the night. I stayed in case he did, but Arnie slept right through. I think he’s still asleep.”

Mandy walked over to examine the patient. A look of alarm sprang onto her face. She grabbed his wrist and then placed a finger on his neck. “Arnie’s dead!”

Shock now hit Paul’s face. “What?! Doc was certain he’d make it.”

“So was I,” Mandy looked at Arnie’s head which was turned. Blotches of vomit clung to his mouth.

The woman smelled a familiar odor. She bent over and sniffed carefully. “Arnie spit up rat poison. He didn’t die from his wounds. He was murdered!”

Chapter Nineteen

The kitchen of Sammy's Hotel and Restaurant was hot, crowded and tense. The Chinese cooks Jenny had introduced as Mr. and Mrs. Toh were nervously preparing a soup. They were being watched by Sammy Wong, Wai Lan, Cal Markham, Buck, and Rance Dehner. Scoop Wilsey stood in the kitchen's open doorway, notebook in hand.

Jenny stood beside the elderly couple, serving as a translator. Mr. Toh whispered softly to Jenny, who spoke directly to the sheriff, "The soup is ready and is identical to what was being served last night."

The young woman ladled some of the soup into a small bowl and handed it to Markham along with a spoon. The lawman sniffed and swallowed the concoction. "It's got a strong taste and smell, reckon it could cover rat poison." He looked at Sammy, "Where did ya say ya keep the poison?"

"In closet behind front desk, along with brooms, mops and cleaning liquids."

"Well, only the soup carried to Arnie was poisoned, since no one who ate here last night has died."

Sammy smiled politely. "As you say, no one die from eating soup last night, this is correct though obvious. However, cause of unfortunate death of Arnie is still very open to speculation."

The mayor's words seemed to anger Cal Markham but he let it pass. "Missus, ah, Lan, are you sure no one handled the soup after the cook gave it to ya?"

"I am certain, Sheriff Markham. Last night, I carried soup directly to the patient."

Jenny spoke to the cooks, telling them they could return full time to preparing food for the breakfast crowd. "We are very busy here," she said to the rest of the group. "If there is nothing more we can do to help—"

A loud raspy voice cut her off. "Too many cooks spoil the stew!"

"Na, Bernie, ya mean too many chinks spoil the stew!"

"Or maybe I shoulda said, poison the stew!"

The two newcomers were standing behind Scoop Wilsey. They were red eyed, unshaven, and appeared to have slept off a drunk outdoors.

The sheriff's response came quick. "You gents best move along 'fore you git into trouble."

Bernie pulled a gun and waved it in the air. "I jus' don't feel much like movin' along, Sheriff. This here gun may be old and rusty but let me tell ya, I kin—"

A large hand grabbed the gun, and another grabbed the back of Bernie's collar. "You tramps are holding up my breakfast," Bill Connors proclaimed, as he stuck the gun in his belt. "I think you can both do with a bit of fresh air."

Connors then clamped his free hand on the arm of Bernie's pal and walked them both out of Sammy's Hotel and Restaurant. When he returned, he received a thank you from Sammy and his daughter along with an assurance that, "You sure make great copy," from Scoop. The newsman scribbled something in his notebook, then bolted for the newspaper office.

Both lawmen gave the boxer a two fingered salute as they departed. Rance Dehner made an identical gesture from a table where he was waiting for Stacey Hooper to join him.

None of those words or signs seemed to make Bruiser Bill Connors happy. He quickly stepped to the table where his agent, Roscoe Platt, was seated.

"Let's step outside for a few minutes, I need to talk to you."

"Sure, Bill, but we can wait until after breakfast. We've got ourselfs all day to talk."

"Now!"

Anger flashed in Roscoe's eyes. Bill Connors was about to throw some harsh words his way and the agent planned to retaliate.

Outside, the two men stepped off the boardwalk as if symbolically starting a street fight. Connors threw the first punch. "I saw you talkin' to them saddle bums a few minutes ago. You put 'em up to causin' trouble, didn't you? Probably gave 'em a quarter a' piece to buy a beer."

"You bet I did! While you were sleeping last night, I was keeping my ear to the ground. Ever'one is all happy 'cause the Chinese dolly got rescued. That's bad for business. We want jaspers to hate the chinks and show up tomorrow to watch you clobber Mack Wong. This morning there's talk about the soup being poisoned by a chink. Poison what killed a white man. No harm in throwing kerosene on the fire."

Platt pulled a cigar out of his coat pocket, bit off the end, and took his time lighting it. As the agent blew out his first cloud of smoke, Bill Connors realized his agent wielded a cigar as a sign of authority, almost using it as a weapon.

Roscoe admired the smoke as it slowly dissipated, then continued. "Besides, I plan on having another autograph signing this afternoon. With people thinking the chinks are out to kill 'em, we'll do a booming business."

"We promised Sammy Wong we'd check with him 'fore doin' another autograph signin'."

"My, my, aren't you becoming the little church mouse! Look, your boxing days are almost over. If you keep boxing, in a few years you'll be nothing but a punch drunk moron who needs help finding the privy. We gotta make all the money we can on this tour and if that means kicking dust on some chinks, so be it."

Connors stared at his agent and wondered when the change had begun. Roscoe Platt was once a fun-loving man, always thinking up crazy ways to sell tickets. When did the fun become desperation, the craziness sink into the mud?

"I know your address, Roscoe."

Platt looked quizzical and worried. "Whatta ya mean?"

"You're not my agent anymore. Git out. I'll mail you your cut from tomorrow's fight."

Roscoe began to flail his hand in the air. The cigar no longer appeared to symbolize power as thin lines of smoke quickly vanished. "You've gone nuts! Who's gonna be your second?"

"I don't need a second. I can splash water on myself."

"A thirty-eight year old boxer, you'll never find another agent."

Bill Connors' eyes glazed, he seemed to be talking half to himself. "I won't be needing an agent. Tomorrow will be the last fight for both Mack Wong and me. I wish I'd had the sense to quit at his age."

"You don't know what you're getting into," Platt's voice was low and bitter. "Nobody gives a damn about an expug. You're gonna be a man alone. I'm leaving on the noon stage. You think I wasn't nice to the chinks. Okay, I hope Mack Wong beats your brains out. Goodbye!"

Bill Connors stood in the street as his former

agent stormed into the hotel to pack his belongings. People had been standing around on the boardwalk listening to the argument. Now they quickly walked off pretending to have heard and seen nothing.

Bruiser Bill Connors sighed deeply and admitted to himself Roscoe had been right about one thing. He felt very alone.

Chapter Twenty

He placed the blade back in its sheath and stared at the clean-shaven image in the mirror. "After this job, I'll grow a beard again," the killer said to himself.

He removed the mirror from the rock on which it perched, returned it to his saddle bag, then put on a shirt. The campfire was completely extinguished. "A body would have to look real careful to know anybody been here last night," The killer again spoke to himself. He frequently did.

Before mounting his sorrel, the man checked his waist. The holster was not tied low. Nothing in his appearance would indicate his profession.

He mused that his latest job was the best kind. He preferred the calling of assassin to that of gunfighter: a lot less risky.

Riding toward Grayson, the assassin mused that this client seemed smarter than most. So many of the people who hired him made demands about riding into town under the cover of darkness. Some cover. Sheriffs and deputies making their rounds always took careful notice of a stranger arriving in the dead of night.

"You can ride right down main street in daytime, and no one looks at you twice. Besides, there are a lotta strangers in Grayson right now with the fight bein' tomorra."

The assassin admitted to himself he was excited about the boxing match. He had read plenty about Bruiser Bill Connors but had never actually seen him in action.

He reined up in the spot where he had been directed. His knock on the front door was immediately answered. He spoke as previously arranged, "Howdy, my name is Lang. I'm new in town and need directions."

The man who now called himself Lang was motioned inside and taken to a small room. There he was handed an envelope containing five hundred dollars. An identical envelope would be his after the job was successfully completed. Instructions were given about where to meet for the final payment.

Of course, there were still details not yet nailed down as to how the job would be carried out. He was to return tomorrow morning at ten, two hours before the fight, for a final explanation of how he would fulfill his responsibility. Lang didn't even try to hide his amusement. His clients always used words like job or responsibility. They never said killing. They were all agreeable about paying for a murder but none of them would speak out loud about death.

After leaving his client, Lang began a careful stroll through Grayson. He needed to know the town well. Once shots were fired and a corpse on the ground, it was impossible to know exactly what would happen next. A good knowledge of the town was essential. He needed to be flexible.

The task proved pleasant. People were continuing to stream into town for the fight. Strangers were everywhere and he became anonymous. He ate a pleasant lunch at Sammy's Hotel and Restaurant. The young Chinese woman who waited on him was a real looker, but Lang was polite to her and nothing more. The gal would flit through his dreams for a while, but he didn't want the lady remembering him.

After lunch, he ambled toward the far north side of town where the church was located. Lang was not interested in the church but in the area about fifty feet in front of it where the boxing match would take place. The assassin was impressed. An actual boxing ring had been set up. People were already gathering around to gawk at the structure, which Lang, a fan of the sweet science, could tell stood in exactly the right proportions.

But the crowd couldn't get too close to the ring. A rope had been tied, fence-like, around it. In fact, ropes had been tied all over the place separating rows of chairs and benches. Tomorrow at noon, nobody would get a place to watch the fight without first buying a ticket.

Two beefy Chinese men patrolled the area. They were wearing Smith and Wessons on their hips and placid expressions on their faces. Their demeanor was casual, obviously regular citizens temporarily employed as guards. As a matter of caution, Lang departed after a few minutes. In a group of mostly harmless appearing family folks, he might stand out.

Lang returned to the town and resumed his appraisal. A group of people were gathering around the front of Sammy's Hotel and Restaurant. Lang stood at the edge of the group. From newspaper and magazine photos and drawings he recognized Bruiser Bill Connors. Connors was talking with a man who was obviously a reporter.

The newspaper guy was scribbling frantically as Bill talked. "Yeah, Roscoe Platt and me has parted company. Platt had some pretty bad ideas about Asian folks. I say folks are pretty much the same no matter how they look. And, you can print this in your paper, Scoop, the Dragon is a good fighter. I just happen to be better. A fact I plan to prove tomorra at noon!"

The crowd laughed and cheered. Connors waved to them, then hastily retreated into the hotel. Filled with a boyish enthusiasm for seeing the famous fighter in person, Lang continued his stroll around Grayson.

By supper time, Lang had learned everything he could. Most of what he saw backed up what the client had told him. The killer had gotten a good look at the sheriff and deputy. The detective, the one called Dehner, had also been easy enough to spot. Dehner's pal, the gambler, had been the easiest of all. He was stationed at a large table in the Mule Kick Saloon taking bets on the fight.

Lang stopped into Sammy's Hotel and Restaurant for an evening meal. The restaurant was packed and the service slow, but the killer didn't mind. He mused to himself that this would be his final restaurant meal for a while. His next job was a long ride away.

Night was beginning to settle in as the killer finished his supper. Looking out the window, he saw parades of people laughing and chattering as they walked about Grayson. With such obvious cover, he could easily pay another quick visit to the site of tomorrow's fight. He had never before seen such a fine ring constructed outside of a major town.

The festive mood of the crowd began to infect Lang as he strolled back toward the northern side of town. His mood shattered when he saw a figure watching the boxing ring and the crowd and guards around it from a tree near the church. The figure seemed to be trying to hide his presence.

Lang took a few strides closer to have his first impressions confirmed. The figure cowering in the darkness under the tree's branches was wearing a hood. Trouble was about to break out and Lang wanted no part of it.

The killer turned and began to walk briskly back into town. He freed his sorrel from the hitch rail where the steed had been tied, mounted, and began to ride out of Grayson. He had only rounded the first bend in the road out of town when he heard a shot and a woman's scream.

Chapter Twenty-One

Chan and Chee Wong were tired but content guards. They had spent the day keeping an eye on the boxing ring and the surrounding chairs and benches. The brothers were one year apart in age. They were sons of one of Sammy's younger brothers who lived in San Francisco.

Mack had "Americanized" his first name. His cousins hadn't given that matter much thought. They had lived their entire lives in San Francisco's Chinatown, a situation which was about to change.

Both Chan and Chee were using their temporary assignment to buttress their future business plans in Grayson. They had talked with many local citizens who had come to gaze on the boxing ring. Courtesy demanded they also talk with visitors to the town, but they did so with minimal enthusiasm.

As the sun began to set, Chee went to his uncle's establishment to retrieve some lanterns. Sammy gladly provided two lanterns along with advice. "Very good to inform citizens of future business. Mention name of business to be Chan and Chee Laundry. Locals find name to have charm. But caution required. Do not let future customer think you start laundry because they are too lazy to clean clothes."

"I tell them truth, Uncle. Grayson has no laundry. Therefore, easier to get business than in San Francisco."

Sammy's eyebrows raised. "Truth sometimes needs polish. Tell citizens you come to Grayson because you prefer it to noise and clamor of San Francisco."

A gleam of understanding filled Chee's eyes. He thanked his uncle and hurried back to the site of the next day's boxing match with the lanterns.

There were still a few dozen people wandering around the roped off area when Chee returned. He stepped over the first rope and placed the lanterns on one of the chairs. Chan was telling an elderly couple that they were starting a laundry in Grayson because of the lack of competition. Chee would soon talk to his brother concerning the art of polishing the truth.

Before he lit the lanterns, Chee began to look about for the best locations to place them. Some place where light would fall on the boxing ring . . .

A shot sounded. A woman screamed as part of the crowd began to run and others froze. Chee and Chan were momentarily stunned. They had been using their status as guards to promote their business. Neither man had given any thought to dealing with serious trouble.

A second shot sent the remaining people in the crowd screaming and running toward town. The two guards ducked under the ropes and hustled to a location away from the chairs which afforded a good view of their surroundings. They drew their guns and hit the ground.

"I think shots came from somewhere near church," Chee said.

Chan cocked his .44. "There is a man moving around there now."

"Do not fire. I think that man stepped from out of the church. He is probably the preacher."

Preacher Paul stood in front of the church, a Colt in his right hand. Whoever had fired the shots could still be lurking in the darkness. The preacher spotted nothing but could hear a wild, maniacal laughter becoming increasingly faint. The gunman was making his way into town.

Paul Colten holstered his gun and began to run toward the sheriff's office. He had reached the first boardwalk when he encountered Cal Markham and Rance Dehner running toward him. All three men stopped.

"What happened?" Markham barked.

Colten paused for a moment to collect his thoughts. "I think someone was firing at the crowd near the boxing ring from the tree near the front of the church. I'm sure he was firing a pistol. I don't think anyone was hurt. I heard him running into town. He was laughing!"

"Did ya see the guy?" the sheriff asked.

"No."

Dehner crunched his face in confusion. "Firing at a crowd from that distance meant he had no one person in mind to shoot."

Colten replied quickly. "Yeh, but he could sure create fear and panic."

Another shot sounded, followed by terrified screams. The three men ran toward the center of town where the commotion was morphing into loud cries for help. Doc Ackerman's buggy momentarily covered them in a dust cloud as it flew by. Ackerman had been returning to Grayson from a call when he heard the explosion of gunfire and a panicked mob.

Dust clouds hadn't yet settled when the three men arrived in front of Bascomb's Emporium where a restless crowd squirmed, cried, cursed, and rambled about as if in boiling water. Dehner and his companions made their way to the middle of the chaos. The crowd had divided in two. Between the two groups, Doc Ackerman was crouched over a child.

"Roger Bascomb!" Preacher Paul exclaimed in a whisper as he went down on one knee beside the boy. "What happened, Roger?"

Roger's head and shoulders were resting in his mother's lap. The boy's father, Ted Bascomb stood at the boy's feet, watching Doctor Ackerman's cautious movements as he examined the child's left leg.

The boy's face was red and damp. Pain scorched his body but he was fighting the urge to cry. "Wasn't my fault, Preacher."

"Of course not, Roger, just tell us what happened."

"I was helpin' Dad and Mom in the store, like always."

"Yes."

"Old Mr. Creighton needed help puttin' stuff on his wagon. After finishin', he gave me a piece of rock candy like he always does, then pulled out. There were lotsa folks walkin' by the store, ya know with the fight tomorra and . . ."

"Yes," Paul Colten spoke in a low, kind voice. "Tell us what happened next."

"I put the candy in my mouth."

"And then?"

"I heard a shot and I fell down. There weren't no hurt at first but then it started hurtin' somethin' awful."

Sheriff Markham stood behind the pastor. "Did ya see where the shot came from?"

Roger moved his head slightly to where he could look across the street. "Ain't sure but I think it was from the alley."

Markham glanced at the alley himself. "Did ya see the gunman?"

"Na."

Fast but irregular footsteps came from across

the street. Buck and Stacey Hooper were running toward the crowd. Their faces were flushed with anger. Both men had witnessed a lot of violence in their lives but had never gotten used to seeing a child shot.

The gambler looked at Dehner as he spoke. "Buck and I were both in the Mule Kick when we heard the shot. When we got here, no one could tell us what the shooter looked like. As soon as the doctor arrived, we both went looking for anyone who looked suspicious—"

"All fer nothin'," Buck cut in. "The town is full a' strangers. Fancy pants and me didn't have a snowball's chance in—" Buck spotted Roger's mom gently caressing her son's forehead, ". . . hades of findin' anythin' unusual. Ain't nothin' usual tonight."

"I must get this boy to my surgery, right now!" The doctor's words came across as an order. The attention of everyone in the crowd suddenly centered on him.

"We need to lift Roger very carefully into my buggy."

Rance, Stacey and Buck complied with the order. The boy gasped in pain only once as they laid him on the driver's seat.

Confusion filled the doc's face as he looked at his patient. With Roger on the seat there was no room for his own bulk.

"I can drive the boy to your house, Doctor."

Mandy Wilsey stepped out of the crowd. Her husband was directly behind her.

"Thank you, Mandy. I will be needing your help tonight."

The young woman nodded assent as she stepped into the buggy, grabbed the reins, and sat on the edge of the seat.

"I'm going too," Roger's mother stepped toward the buggy, then paused, looking for some way to fit into the crowded conveyance.

There was no room for anyone else in the buggy. A moment of confusion rustled through the crowd, but only for a moment. A gangly cowboy placed two fingers on his hat as he approached the distraught woman and pointed to the hitch rail in front of the store. "Mrs. Bascomb, the boys and me tied up our horses here, 'cause we knowed there'd be no space in front of the saloons. We'd be plumb happy if you, your husband, and the doc rode three of them horses right along beside the buggy as Roger goes to git patched up."

Stella Bascomb recognized the cowboy. He was an occasional customer at the store, but she couldn't remember his name and could only stammer, "Thank you so much."

"Don't give no never mind to bringin' them horses back. Jus' leave 'em in front of Doc's house. We kin come and git 'em ourselfs."

As this brief scene played out, Clyde stood

beside the buggy whining and wagging his tail. At one point, he backed up and did a running jump into Mandy's lap. The woman handed the dog to her husband.

Clyde didn't remain with Scoop for long. As the procession took off for the doctor's house, the dog jumped from the reporter's arms and ran behind the buggy. He would once again be beside his mistress as she helped perform a surgery.

Paul Colten spoke before the procession had gone very far. "I need to get over to Doc's house myself. My place is with Roger's parents. If you gents could remember Roger and his family in prayer, that would be appreciated."

"Try to remember us too, Vicar," Stacey requested. "In a town filled with strangers we will be trying to find a ruthless killer. A little divine intervention would definitely be appreciated."

Chapter Twenty-Two

The crowd dispersed, many of them shaking their heads as if shrugging off the horror they had just witnessed. There would be a boxing match tomorrow and a lot of celebrating tonight. Life was hard, you grabbed what fun you could.

Five men huddled in front of Bascomb's Emporium: Rance Dehner, Stacey Hooper, Sheriff Cal Markham, Buck, and Scoop Wilsey. The sheriff spoke first. "This thing makes no damn sense. Why would someone shoot at a group of people from a distance too far away to know who might get hit and then shoot down a boy?"

Dehner's answer was quick. "The big crowd and excitement have pushed a jasper who was crazy to start with, completely over the cliff. He wants the same attention the Dragon and Bruiser Bill Connors are getting. If that means shooting a child, so be it."

"Alcohol has probably given him the courage he needs," Scoop added.

Markham gave a deep sigh. He didn't like what he had just heard but didn't disagree with it. "Gents, let's break up into groups of two and patrol the town. That's all I know to do. Look for anythin' suspicious and do what ya can ta keep the lid on. Dehner, you and the gambler move north, Buck and I will go south, that way we'll cover Main Street where most of the hoorawin' is goin' on."

The sheriff suddenly took note of the newspaperman. "Ah, Wilsey, you tag along with Dehner and his friend."

As Rance and his two companions made their way up the street, Scoop whispered a few mild profanities, then spoke out loud. "I should be used to Sheriff Markham by now. He's never cared much for the *Grayson Herald*, Mandy, me and even Clyde. He's become even more down on the newspaper lately."

"Why is that?" Dehner asked.

"I think the sheriff wants people to forget about the murder of Doc Cranston," Scoop answered. "He doesn't know where to begin to catch the killer. But I'm going to keep the murder front and center in the minds of the good citizens of Grayson."

"Don't let the sheriff's hostility bother you," Stacey's voice, as always, was chirpy. "At least he deigned to mention your name. I was reduced to being 'the gambler' or Rance's 'friend.' Not that I was offended."

Raucous laughter was exploding from only a few yards away. "Why don't you two put your complaints about Sheriff Markham aside," Dehner suggested. "We should visit the Mule Kick. Our man may be seeking more courage.

Markham and Buck will probably come here too. It's the center of town and the center of trouble."

Stacey sounded agreeable. "And maybe the presence of faux lawmen like we three will prevent the customers from indulging in fist fights and even more dangerous endeavors."

As the three men entered the saloon, they received a friendly but quick nod from Jeb. Customers were double lined around the bar. The barkeep was scrambling to keep everyone happy.

"Let's break up and walk around the place," Dehner said. "Listen in to what these jaspers are saying. We may hear something useful."

About fifteen minutes later, the threesome reassembled in front of the Mule Kick's batwings. "I picked up nothing that could help," Dehner admitted. "How about you two?"

Stacey and Scoop both shook their heads. Scoop looked particularly troubled. "Hard to believe, but I spotted several men who were in the crowd watching Roger Bascomb bleed and his mother cry. Now, they're making lewd jokes, getting drunk and pawing the saloon girls."

"A shame Preacher Paul isn't here," Stacey said.

"Why?" Scoop asked.

Stacey lifted an index finger. "The behavior you witnessed would make excellent examples for a sermon on the lingering power of original sin."

Dehner moved the discussion off theology. “I think we should head up the boardwalk toward Delilah’s.”

Wilsey smirked, then seemed to warm to the detective’s suggestion. “You think our gunman has decided to bed down for the night, or at least bed down for an hour with some company?”

“From what Buck tells me, Delilah, or the madam who calls herself Delilah, cooperates with the law. It might be worth our while.”

As the threesome left the saloon, they heard a shot and a screeching laugh. Dehner looked up the street. “Sounds like it’s coming from the end of the boardwalk, where Delilah’s is located.”

Stacey beamed a smile. “It appears we have another fine example of the power of original sin.”

Dehner broke into a run. The other two men followed.

Chapter Twenty-Two

As the threesome approached Delilah's they spotted a group of about a dozen people standing in the middle of the street and looking upward. Unlike the larger crowd they had been with less than an hour before, this bunch was laughing.

"Let's find out what all the fun's about," Rance suggested. The silliness of the bystanders waned a bit as the three serious looking men joined them to see a hooded figure standing on the roof of the two story Delilah's. He fired a pistol into the air, bellowed a loud laugh, and shouted, "Tomorra, I'll fight both the Dragon and Bruiser Bill. I'll send both of 'em cryin' to their mommies!"

"Do you think that's the man who shot Roger?" Scoop asked.

The question had been directed at Rance, but Stacey answered it. "I would say that his behavior definitely qualifies him as a suspect."

"You two keep an eye on things at ground level," Dehner said. "I'm going to see if I can bring our suspect down to earth."

Rance entered Delilah's, where a short, moon-faced woman wearing a red dress that dragged against the floor gave him a quizzical look. "Whadda ya want?"

"My name's Rance Dehner, I—"

"Buck tole me all 'bout ya. Ya here to clean the roof?"

"Yes. Is there a way onto the—"

"Honey, if ya wanna git on the roof, ya gotta do it like the guy with a sack on his head. Go upstairs to the first room, crawl out the winda and pull yourself up."

"Thanks!"

Dehner began to take the stairs two at a time. Delilah shouted after him. "Make sure ya use the first door. The other rooms are bein' used by customers."

"Don't worry, I wouldn't want to interrupt commerce."

Arriving on the second floor, Dehner barged through the first door. A slightly pudgy woman with lipstick on her chin sat on a bed which was the room's only furniture.

She smiled in a way that made it look like work. "Looking for a little fun, handsome?"

"I guess you could put it that way." Dehner moved toward the room's one window.

Intensity suddenly filled the woman's voice. "You're after that creep!"

Rance looked out the window, which afforded only a slight view of the flat roof. "He's a lot worse than a creep."

"I'll say!" The woman sprang from the bed and continued to talk to the detective as he climbed out the window. "Sack Head ran in the front door, pushed Delilah aside, high tailed it up here and barged in. Delilah follows him waving a pistol. Sack Head got out the window 'fore she could shoot. All the ruckus scared off a paying customer. When you catch the snake, tell him he owes . . ."

The woman's voice became fainter as Dehner grasped the edge of the roof and slowly pulled himself up. He had no idea where Sack Head, as the women called him, was located.

As his eyes moved over the roof, Dehner spotted a dark shape moving about in a pit of blackness created by weak moonlight. Rance climbed onto the roof as the shape shouted to the crowd below.

"I'll jus' beat up on Bruiser Bill, but I'll kill the chink and send him to hell."

A barrage of voices sounded from the street, some friendly, others hostile. Rance began to move toward his adversary, who once again fired a gun harmlessly into the air.

A solitary, loud voice sounded from below. "You got company up there, pal!"

The hooded shape turned and gave a loud screech like a mountain lion warning off a predator. To Dehner's surprise, the outlaw holstered his gun and ran to the side of the roof where he jumped onto the neighboring hardware store.

Despite himself, the detective was impressed.

The jump was about five yards and downward onto the single-level store. Yet, his adversary had landed cat-like on the store's flat roof.

"Maybe he really is a mountain lion." Dehner spoke cynically to himself before also making the jump and landing a short distance behind his prey.

Sack Head drew his gun and once again sent a bullet on a doomed journey toward the clouds. Still crouched in a landing position, Dehner pulled his Colt as Sack Head gave a playful laugh and fired downward toward the crowd.

A painful scream was followed by angry shouts. "Not again!" Sack Head's voice resounded with hurt and confusion. He yelled curses at a fate which was treating him so unfairly.

The hooded figure turned and spotted Dehner's Colt pointing at him. The outlaw dropped his own gun and made a dash for the side of the store. Only a few feet beside the store was a one story freight company with a peaked roof. Compared to the outlaw's previous jump this task looked easy.

But the jump ended in disaster. The outlaw's head collided with the freight company's side wall and he dropped to the ground.

"Stay here!" the voice belonged to Sherrif Cal Markham. Rance couldn't see who he was addressing.

Dehner watched from above. Markham's

words had come through fast erratic breaths. The lawman had heard all the commotion from the other end of town and run to the trouble. Cal looked upwards and yelled, "Can you see our friend, Rance?"

"No. The alley's too dark. He may be unarmed. He left one gun up here."

Markham drew his own gun. He quickly stepped out of the weak yellow light which overlapped from the lantern hanging over Delilah's and moved into total darkness.

A noise sounding not quite like a gunshot sounded behind Dehner. A sallow face with sunken cheeks protruded from an open square in the roof. The newcomer held up a lantern revealing a trap door now laying open in front of him.

"Been listening to all the hoorawing," the man said. "When I heard you talking to the sheriff, I figgered you was a good man. My name is Marvin; I own the store."

Dehner ran to the trap door. Marvin began to slowly descend a ladder downward. Rance closed the trap door and followed the store owner. But the detective couldn't rush downward. Marvin seemed more interested in conversation than getting to the bottom of the ladder.

"I live here in the store now," Marvin tried to sound casual, but his words resounded with the desperation of loneliness. "My wife died some years ago. I sold my house last year so my son could go East to college."

Somewhat reluctantly, Marvin stepped off the last rung of the ladder and onto the floor. "You know, times are changing. It's important for a boy to get all the education—"

Dehner nodded a thank you, bolted from the store, and ran to the alley. Cal Markham and Scoop Wilsey had the outlaw's arms around their shoulders. They were walking him out of the alley.

"This jasper's name is Jeff Taggert," Scoop pointed toward the outlaw, who's head was now sackless. "Two months ago, he caused some serious damage in the Lucky Trail Saloon. He's been working as a swamper there to help pay for all the destruction."

"Ya put my name in the paper for doin' it." Jeff slurred his words. His head was bleeding and his limp appeared genuine.

"Where's Stacey?" Rance asked.

Cal angrily glanced at the man he was helping. "This fool shot someone else while he was up there on the roof. Thank God, it wasn't a kid. Your friend helped git up a group to carry the poor jasper to Doc Ackerman's."

"We're taking Taggert there now," Scoop added. "Doc and Mandy are sure having a busy night."

"They'll treat this fool last," Sheriff Cal Markham declared.

• • •

On the way to the doctor's house, Markham explained to his two companions that he and Buck had been breaking up a fight between four drunks when they heard commotion coming from the opposite end of town. His deputy had remained to disarm the drunks. "Buck will hear the quiet comin' from this end and reckon we got our thumb on it. He's keepin' an eye on the south side."

As they stepped into Doctor Ackerman's surgery, they witnessed a scene of quiet intensity. Ackerman was bent over Roger, who was lying on a large table, while the boy's parents and Preacher Paul stood nearby. A few feet from the table, Mandy was applying a bandage to the wounded arm of a man lying on one of the three beds.

Markham spoke to the room, "We've got the rat who shot the boy and the gent, where—"

Stacey approached the newcomers like the head waiter in an exclusive restaurant. "Always room for another customer. We have a vacant bed," he pointed his finger to the object running along the far wall. "Please help our most recent arrival to the accommodations and see that he is made comfortable."

Dehner spoke to his friend in a whisper as Scoop and the sheriff carried out Stacey's instructions. "How's Roger?"

Stacey's reply was also a whisper and more serious than his greeting. "They've got the bullet out and will sew him up when Mandy is finished attending to that wretched villain's other victim. Roger will not lose the leg. Otherwise, the doctor can't say for sure, but he is optimistic that the boy will eventually regain full use of his leg."

"And the other victim?" Rance asked.

"A very fortunate fellow. The bullet didn't hit anything vital, just ripped his shoulder."

Mandy Wilsey hurried by Rance and Stacey to look at the recently arrived patient. Clyde followed at her heels. The woman crouched over Taggert and spoke to her husband. "There's a stack of cloths and bandages by the sink. Wash the head wound, then bandage it. We'll look at him after we've done everything we can for Roger."

Mandy returned to helping Doctor Ackerman. Clyde pattered behind her, then laid down on the floor near her feet. Scoop followed his wife's instructions. He didn't speak to Taggert until the bandage was on. "That will stop the bleeding. Lay down, the doc will get to you when he can."

Scoop walked over to Rance, Stacey and the sheriff. The three men had been huddled together, all of them aware very important things were going on but not knowing how to help.

The newspaperman pulled a notebook and pencil from his jacket pocket. He looked back at the man he had just bandaged and casually asked, "Jeff Taggert, I know your name was in the paper before but I forgot, is that 'Jeff' with a J or a G?"

"Make it a J," came the response. "The story is gonna read, Jeff Taggert Escapes!"

Taggert rose from his bed unsteadily, a Derringer in his right hand. "Everbody jus' stay put. I don't wanna shoot no more—"

Stella Bascomb yelled frantically, "You've already shot my boy, what kind of man are you?!"

Taggert turned to the woman. "Ma'am, I didn't wanna hurt—"

Cal Markham's hand created a blur as he drew his gun and punched a bullet into Taggert's chest. The outlaw plunged backward, his legs colliding with the bed and his head slamming against the back wall.

Stella screamed, Mandy gasped, and Tom Bascomb embraced his wife. Everyone in the room stood frozen as they watched Taggert's falling body bounce against the side of the bed before colliding with the floor.

Markham ran to the fallen outlaw and grabbed the Derringer. "Damn!" he said in a loud whisper, then grabbed Taggert's wrist. "He's dead."

Cal looked apologetically at Tom and Stella Bascomb. "This is my fault." He held up the Derringer. "I shoulda' checked the jasper better than I did."

Stella closed her eyes briefly, then looked at

the lawman. "What kind of town is Grayson? I mean . . ."

Markham's voice was firm. "Grayson is the kind of town where if a snake shoots a boy, he pays the price. Fast."

Doc Ackerman spoke calmly. "As soon as I finish here—"

Sheriff Markham cut him off. "You got important work ta do, Doc. There's plenty of extra hands here. We can take out the trash."

Chapter Twenty-Three

The assassin now named Lang experienced a surge of joy and excitement as he rode into Grayson. He lived for the days when he killed.

He dismounted and tied up his horse in the same location where he had met his client the day before. Lang wasn't surprised to see curtains fluttering in the window and the front door opening before he reached it.

Once again, the killer was taken to the small room and there given instructions as to where and how to carry out his "responsibilities." Lang replied in a low, guttural voice, "I ain't the only one who's gotta act responsible. You better be at the location with the rest of my money. I don't got much patience for people who aren't responsible. No patience at all."

The client responded as they all do, spraying out words like "Yes, yes, of course." Words made sporadic by a quivering body.

Outside again and mounting his horse, Lang wondered when killing had become so important to him. He had begun to kill for the easy money. He was good with a gun and could have been a lawman making forty dollars a month, sixty in some places. A thousand dollars was now his going price and there were enough people willing to pay it.

But it really wasn't the money, not anymore. The only important thing was knowing that by the end of the day, a man would be lying dead because of him. Being a carrier of death thrilled him.

Sure, he passed time now and again with booze and women. But those diversions provided less and less enjoyment. And Lang could still get some fun from a boxing match or a baseball game. He was modestly surprised at how seeing Bruiser Bill had amused him.

As his horse plodded into the center of Grayson, the killer wondered at how some gunfighters thought their reputations were so important. Hell, a reputation is nothing but a rope you tie around yourself. A reputation means you can't shoot a man in the back or ambush him.

The killer laughed softly to himself. "Some jaspers worry over the damnedest things." He laughed again. Lang was experiencing absolute joy.

As previously arranged, Mack Wong stepped into the boxing ring first. His appearance was met with both boos and applause. Mack was a bit surprised. He was expecting only boos, but then recalled the large number of Asians who had come into town for the fight.

Mack took off his robe leaving him naked to the waist. He began to stretch both his arms and legs.

He was nimble despite the tight fitting pants.

Barry and Peter Thomas appeared at the same time Mack did but never entered the ring. Peter carried a water bucket and a small case containing iodine and a few other aids that could close a cut.

Peter set the medicine case on a small table directly behind the ring which had been placed there for that purpose. He set the bucket down beside the table.

Peter grabbed the robe Mack had left on the ring's top rope. He looked at the front row where the Wong family was seated and handed the robe to Jenny. "Hold it tight, you'll bring your cousin good luck."

The couple exchanged a few silly remarks. Sammy Wong, seated beside his daughter, watched with an expressionless face. Sammy liked and approved of Peter Thomas, but it was too early to let anyone know it.

A loud cheer broke out from the crowd as Bruiser Bill Connors entered from the opposite side of the ring. The fighter was carrying his own bucket and case which he hastily attended to, then holding the top rope on the ring, he jumped over it. The cheering grew louder followed by yells of encouragement.

Sammy Wong smiled mischievously and whispered to his daughter. "Bruiser Bill very fortunate. Unlike honorable nephew, Bill only hear cheers. Asians in attendance all too polite to boo."

Jenny broke out in laughter and received a harsh stare from her Auntie Wai Lan. The young woman stopped laughing but continued to be grateful for her father's sense of humor.

Mack Wong was not in a humorous mood. He went into his corner and motioned for both Thomas men to join him.

"Bill Connors was carrying his own bucket and medicine case. There is no one to handle his robe for him. Why?" the young fighter asked.

"Didn't ya hear?" Barry Thomas snapped. "Connors got in an argument with his two-bit manager. Roscoe Platt took off like a coyote smelling a dead cow. Connors is on his own."

Mack quickly pointed across the ring. "Peter, I want you to serve as Mr. Connors' second."

"What?! I'll be helping your opponent to—"

"You will be sponging him off a bit and preventing bruises from opening up," Mack explained calmly. "If that is all he requires to defeat me, then he deserves victory. Please get over there immediately."

As Peter followed instructions, Mack looked at the patrons on the other side of the ring. "I have family sitting nearby. The people who are sitting near Bill Connors and cheering him are strangers. Bill will never see them again."

The older Thomas gave a harsh laugh. "Don't

waste sympathy on that pug. Hell, he us'ta be surrounded by friends, especially female friends."

"He was surrounded by people," Mack said. "But they were not friends. They were strangers and they have forgotten him."

Bill Connors watched with hostile curiosity as Peter did a fast inspection of the older fighter's medicine case, water bucket and even noted Bill's robe now folded and lapping over the table containing the case. Those tasks accomplished, Peter stepped onto the edge of the ring. "Hello Bill, I'm your second."

The reply was angry. "I don't need a second, and I don't need charity, now get outta here!"

Peter's voice was strong and business like. "This isn't charity, it's common sense. If a cut over your eye starts to bleed, you may not notice it until red blurs your vision of Mack coming at you. I'm here to stop that."

Connors inhaled deeply, looked at something only he could see, then nodded his head in agreement. "Hot as hell today," he said to his second.

"Probably in the nineties."

Bill wiped off the sweat already lining his forehead. "They always have outdoor boxing matches at noon, so the sun don't get in the fighters eyes. I'd rather put up with a little glare if the temperature was decent."

Peter agreed and felt a bit more comfortable. Bill Connors seemed to have accepted him.

Preacher Paul climbed in the ring through a neutral corner, walked to the center and began to address the crowd. “Ladies and gentlemen, boys and girls, welcome to fifteen rounds of boxing. In this corner . . .”

As the preacher introduced the boxers, the crowd’s reaction was identical to when the fighters first entered. Mack received a mixed response while Bruiser Bill heard only cheers. Sammy Wong smiled approvingly; the Asians were maintaining their courtesy.

Peter Thomas watched Connors once again soak in the loud applause and encouraging shouts from the crowd. It was a curiously strange sight. Bruiser Bill’s body appeared to take on new strength. The man who returned to his corner looked ten years younger.

Preacher Paul, in his position of referee, motioned both men to the center of the ring. “You gentlemen both know the rules. I won’t repeat them, but rest assured I will enforce them. Go to your corners and come out boxing.”

As the two fighters carried out instructions, Paul Colten looked at the threesome sitting close to a neutral corner of the ring. Ted Bascomb held a stopwatch. Roger Bascomb, excited and happy despite his pale complexion, sat beside his father holding a cow bell. Stella sat on her son’s other side, looking concerned but joyful over Roger's obvious excitement and happiness.

Preacher Paul pointed a finger at the boy, who then loudly rang the bell. Both fighters jumped off their stools and advanced to the center of the ring.

The first four rounds went as predicted. Mack Wong delivered a few hard jabs to Connors' ribs and arms. He managed to deliver two blows to Connors' head but only one had any force behind it. Wong's strategy was to keep moving fast and make the older boxer come after him. It seemed to be working. Connors couldn't get close enough to his opponent to land a damaging blow.

By the fifth round, the heat was beginning to get to the fans as well as to the fighters. The crowd wanted a direct brutal confrontation and began to shout out their displeasure.

During the sixth round, the situation turned ugly. One loutish barfly with leather lungs jumped to his feet and shouted, "You're yella in more ways than one, Wong!" A chunk of the crowd exploded in laughter and applause.

Mack became infuriated and foolish. He moved directly toward his opponent.

Lightning flashed in Mack Wong's head. His vision blurred and his legs turned to rubber. He danced back not very gracefully as Bill Connors came after him poised to deliver a crushing second haymaker that would end the fight.

Mack realized he was moving into the ropes. If Bruiser Bill trapped him there the match would be over. All those mornings of running paid off. Strength returned to Wong's legs. He ducked down and quickly side stepped around Connors.

But Bruiser Bill was determined to end the fight. Arms ready to deliver another hard blow, he rapidly advanced on his weakened opponent.

The bell rang.

Both fighters returned to their corners. Bruiser Bill received words of encouragement from his second. Peter Thomas was both surprised and amused by how easy it was for him to switch allegiances.

Peter suddenly recalled he was going to use the money he would win from betting on Mack to buy a fine wedding ring for Jenny. But then, he hadn't proposed to her yet.

"One thing at a time," the young man said aloud.

"Whatta ya mean?" Connors asked

"I mean . . . after you knock Mack out, we'll all celebrate!"

Bruiser Bill smiled as Peter sponged him down.

Mack Wong heard no words of encouragement. Barry Thomas snapped angrily at the fighter as he almost collapsed onto his stool. "You jus' gave everyone a fine example of bein' saved by the bell."

Mack nodded his head. A rare look of anger

appeared on his face. Anger directed at himself. "I let a fool direct my actions. It will not happen again."

The seventh round was a bit of a humiliation for Mack Wong. Still woozy and unsure of himself, he spent the round staying away from his opponent.

But by the eighth round, Wong was back in form. He confidently pounded Connors' body while not allowing his opponent the opportunity for another haymaker.

Wong's punches to Connors' arms began to reap a strong benefit by the tenth round. Bill Connors was holding those arms noticeably lower. Mack took advantage. Two hard punches to Connors' ribs caused the older fighter to widen the gap between his arms. Mack responded with a vicious uppercut.

Bill Connors staggered backwards as a sharp pain flamed in Mack's right hand. But the younger fighter realized his chance was now. He jabbed Connors' head with a hard left, then used his injured hand to deliver a sledgehammer blow.

Connors went down. He tried to get back onto his feet but failed. On a second attempt he made it onto his hands and knees but could get no further. In that position he heard Preacher Paul reach the count of ten and declare him out.

Paul lifted Mack Wong's hand, officially indicating Mack had won the fight. A loud cacophony of noise seemed to rise from the crowd and ascend into the clouds.

"Are you going to miss all this?" Paul asked the victor.

"Yes," came the truthful reply. Mack Wong then looked toward his opponent's corner. Connors was on his feet. Peter was sponging Bill's face which was gray with defeat.

"But there are some things about boxing I will not miss," Mack added. He walked over to shake Bill's hand.

Chapter Twenty-Four

Buck and Stacey Hooper were part of the pick-up crew moving tables to the side of the Mule Kick Saloon for the town celebration about to take place.

"I reckon you're used ta all this, Fancy Pants."

Stacey noted that Buck's use of Fancy Pants was sounding more friendly than mocking. The two men had spent the last several hours working together, along with Rance Dehner, at trying to prevent a murder. A certain *esprit de corps* had been established.

"No, Buck, I've always thought moving tables and chairs to be a task best left to the working class."

Buck chortled as he and Stacey dropped a round table near one of the saloon's side walls and began scooting chairs under it. "What I meant was, don't ya English folks have a holiday called Boxing Day? Must be a lotta hoorawing over the fights on that day."

"In England, Boxing Day is the day after Christmas."

"Makes sense," Buck declared. "After all that jawin' 'bout goodwill an' peace on earth, folks like to watch two jaspers try to knock each other's brains out."

"Not exactly," Stacey replied. "I believe that on Boxing Day one is supposed to box up old items no longer needed and take them to the poor."

Buck looked startled. "Do folks really do that?"

"No."

"Then, why—"

To Stacey's relief, Doctor Richard Ackerman's voice thundered over the saloon. "Our guests of honor are coming, folks. Let's get ready to greet them!"

Excited whispers cascaded over the Mule Kick. The large crowd was hardly typical of the customers who were usually found in the saloon. Women and children made up a large portion of those present. The atmosphere was one of a church picnic.

Bill Connors and Mack Wong stepped into the Mule Kick together. They both seemed surprised by the loud applause they received.

Connors spoke softly to his former opponent. "I gotta tip my hat to these folks. After all, a lot of them jus' lost money bettin' on me."

The moment the applause began to subside, Richard Ackerman's voice thundered once again. "The editor of the *Grayson Herald*, Scoop Wilsey, informs me that his account of the fight will appear in papers across the nation. I say, let's give those folks more than just words. Let's also send them a picture of these two great boxers!"

Quiet excitement filled the saloon. People

sensed they were a part of history as Mack and Bill stood at military attention while Scoop prepared to take their picture. Even Clyde, standing dutifully beside Scoop, remained silent and still. The newspaperman expertly manipulated his Pearsall into the best position, then took the picture. Applause followed.

Edward Ackerman was intent on moving things along. He motioned for the Wong family who had been waiting on the other side of the batwings along with the two Thomases to come in. He shouted for everyone to find a chair as he escorted the newcomers to the long table that ran along the front of the bar.

When everyone was seated, the doctor resumed his role as master of ceremonies. He stood at the center of the table and gestured to the man seated at his right. "Mayor Wong, we are all about to enjoy a delicious meal provided by your restaurant. Since you are charging us no money for the food, I don't think you will receive many complaints."

After laughing at his own joke, Ackerman continued. "I will admit that this whole affair was my idea. We would have held it no matter who won the fight. Not many towns would have done so, but Grayson is someplace special."

Ackerman gripped his jacket, indicating he was about to get to the point. "At the last election, this town elected as mayor a man who came to this country many years ago. He started his life in this new land by helping to build the railroad. He has served this town well as illustrated by the fact that he brought a great athletic event to Grayson. Let us all show our appreciation for our great mayor, Sammy Wong."

Applause once again exploded in the Mule Kick. Sammy smiled and whispered to his nephew, who was sitting beside him, "Unlike boxer, Sammy not hear any boos. Free food brings great courtesy."

The doctor kept his hand on his coat. He was still being serious. "The food will be brought out in a moment. First, I will ask Pastor Paul Colten to come forward and lead us in prayer."

Doctor Ackerman scooted off to make way for Preacher Paul.

Lang had long before honed the skill of looking casual as he prepared to take down another target. That skill didn't seem necessary on this day. The town appeared deserted. If it had not been for the voices blaring out of the Mule Kick Saloon, Grayson could have been mistaken for a ghost town.

Out of habit, Lang maintained his relaxed pose as he tied his horse at the rail in front of the Mule Kick. He gave what appeared to be an indifferent glance toward the saloon's large front window.

Drawing his Peacemaker, Lang stepped quickly

toward the window. His eyes centered on the soon to be victim.

"Drop the gun!" Rance Dehner sprang out from the alley beside the Mule Kick, Colt in hand.

The detective's vision was fixed on the hired killer. Only luck and an anxious assailant caused the bullet being fired from across the street to fly inches over Dehner's head.

Rance dropped to the ground and rolled into the alley. Lang, the plan in ruins, mounted his horse and galloped off.

Shouts, screams and general clamor came from inside the Mule Kick. Buck and Stacey Hooper, guns drawn, broke through the batwings.

Dehner stared across the street at the rain barrel in the alley. A familiar face peeked over that barrel. Jeb Smith fired another shot in Dehner's direction then rose and started to run. Rance returned fire. Jeb's run ended. He yelled in pain before he stumbled and fell. The barkeep then squirmed in the dirt, whining for help.

The detective quickly rose to his feet and ran for his bay which was also tethered to the rail in front of the Mule Kick.

"Want me and Fancy Pants to ride with ya?"

"No, Buck," Dehner spoke as he mounted the bay. "There's plenty that needs doing right here. Remember what I told you."

Those last words were almost lost in the pounding hoofbeats of Dehner's horse.

Chapter Twenty-Five

The trail outside of Grayson was flat. Rance Dehner assumed his prey was galloping straight ahead. There were no side trails to take, and the surrounding rocky ground could render a horse lame.

After less than ten minutes, Dehner spotted a slowly dissipating pall of dust up ahead. His bay seemed to be enjoying the fast run as the animal's powerful legs shortened the distance between the detective and the fleeing outlaw. But the heat was sweltering. This speed couldn't be maintained for long.

Rance yanked his bandanna over his nose. But dust blurred his vision as he neared a spot where large cottonwoods on each side of the trail provided a rare haven of shade.

A sense of alarm shot through the detective. A rope had been tied across the trail. Dehner, who had been hunched over the bay's neck, stood up in the stirrups and shifted his weight backwards as he shouted "jump!"

From a distance the scene might have looked funny. The bay followed orders to an absurd degree, sailing gracefully over the rope which had been tied across the trail to the bottom of two trees.

But Dehner wasn't in a humorous mood. Not with a killer working to outsmart him. He whisked his Winchester from the saddle's scabbard, then did a quick slide off the horse and scurried behind a boulder that protruded from one side of the trail.

The detective quickly looked around him as he pulled down the bandanna. There was only one tree on the side of the trail where he was hiding and a few scraggly brown bushes. The large rock he stood behind provided the only cover.

The other side of the trail was almost identical only with a line of smaller boulders surrounding a large boulder. Dehner examined those smaller stones carefully. They would provide cover for a man in a crouch or on his knees.

Dehner wondered if he hadn't been played for a fool. The snake who almost committed murder in Grayson was a professional. After tying a rope across the trail, he might be still riding off, confident that anyone chasing him was now limping about getting ready to shoot his crippled horse.

Probably not, Rance thought. Tying that rope across the trail caused the outlaw to lose valuable time. If the trick didn't work, the lawman chasing him would be that much closer. Dehner figured the killer had reckoned on just one pursuer. Posses take a while to form.

The rat was in hiding. He had hoped his

adversary would be violently tossed from his steed and in an excellent place for an ambush. That plan had been foiled but only slightly. The killer still had his enemy in sight.

Dehner needed to locate the outlaw. He looked carefully at the thick tree that stood on the other side of the trail. If someone was standing behind it, they were standing at military attention and standing absolutely still. Unlikely.

Rance smiled inwardly as the obvious became obvious to him. The thick branches covered with leaves on both trees provided excellent cover. If the killer's first plan didn't work, a tree would provide a fine location for a second try whatever his prey's location.

Rance sighed with relief and gave a silent prayer of thanks. His enemy was probably in the tree across the trail. Dehner chose not to give too much thought to what would have happened if his prey had been in the tree directly beside him.

The scalding heat of the day caused the trees to bow in stillness. Denied any wind, they were unable to move by themselves. Dehner squatted, laid his rifle on the ground, then took off his hat and pretended to wipe his forehead. He didn't look up but shifted his eyes toward the tree branches.

One of the branches moved slightly. Dehner grabbed the Winchester, went into a fast roll which took him past the boulder, then fired a shot toward the rustling leaves. A loud shriek was followed by a red spear that furrowed into the ground and kicked dust on Rance's face.

The detective levered his rifle and sent a second shot toward a target he still couldn't see. The tree branch jerked to one side as the gunman tried to cling to it. A sharp wail of desperation cut the air followed by a moan of defeat.

A blur descended from the tree spraying thick splotches of blood before hitting the ground. Rance sprang to his feet and again levered the Winchester. The killer had landed with a rifle still in his hand.

Lying on the ground, Lang gasped for breath as he pointed the rifle at Dehner. The detective responded with a shot to his enemy's chest.

Lang dropped the rifle and spread out limp on the ground. Dehner watched carefully before moving. The man was still breathing. Dehner ran toward him, kicked his rifle away, then pulled the pistol from the outlaw's holster and tossed it to a safe distance.

The killer looked at Dehner with glassy, moist eyes. "That's jus' the second time I tried that trick. Worked good a few months ago. A U.S. Marshal got trapped under his horse, after the horse tripped and broke his leg." The killer smiled; even under the circumstances, the memory brought him pleasure. "I put both the horse and the marshal outta their misery."

Dehner recognized and understood the quirks of the man he had just shot out of a tree. The killer took pride in his cleverness and had to explain that his plan had once succeeded.

"What's your name?" Dehner spoke quickly. His adversary was slipping away.

A bitter laugh pushed blood over the man's chin. "Right now, I'm called Lang. Been known as Dakota, Hank, . . . Stone . . . ya name it . . . don't make no difference."

"Who hired you, Lang?"

"Ain't never tole who the boss was, never will . . ."

"You're going to be meeting up with God, soon, Lang. No promises, but it might help if you tell me the truth."

"You're wrong. It's Satan I'm meetin' up with. He'll be happier iffen I don't talk. Besides, I never helped no lawman . . . no . . . not . . ."

Blood turned Lang's voice into a gurgle, then his eyes glazed over, and he stopped making any sounds at all.

As he rose to his feet, Rance could hear the neighing of horses coming from down the trail. His bay and the horse belonging to Lang had probably found a small stream somewhere and were enjoying a drink together.

"I could use some water myself," Rance sighed and began to walk toward the horses and the canteen resting on his bay's saddle.

Despite the heat, Rance moved quickly. There was plenty to attend to back in Grayson. His mind began to review the bizarre puzzle he had been piecing together since arriving in Grayson. He didn't have all the parts yet, but . . .

"Stop right there, Dehner!" A familiar voice shouted. "Turn around slow like and keep your hands away from your gun."

Dehner shook his head sadly as he followed orders and faced the rifleman who stood about ten yards away. "I really hoped it wasn't you."

"Sorry to disappoint," said Sheriff Cal Markham.

Chapter Twenty-Six

Anger surged through Rance Dehner. "Markham, the hottest seats in hell are reserved for crooked lawmen."

Cal Markham stepped closer to the detective. "You've been spendin' too much time with Preacher Paul. Now, real slow like, drop that Winchester in front of ya."

The Winchester landed inches in front of Rance's boots. "Okay now, do the same thing for that gun in your holster and then take four steps back."

Once again, Rance reluctantly followed instructions. Markham picked up the Colt and stuck it in his belt. While keeping his rifle aimed at his captive, he tucked the Winchester under his left arm. "Now, we're gonna walk back to where poor Lang is restin' in peace. I figger he's a mite lonely. So, you'll be joinin' him."

Dehner walked forward several feet before Markham began to walk at a safe distance behind him. Rance began to laugh.

"What's sa damn funny?!"

"Only a few minutes ago, I was asking Lang who the boss man was. I already knew. Doc Ackerman is running the show. You're just his errand boy, aren't you, Markham?"

"Shut up and keep walkin'."

Rance gave another good-natured laugh. "When he arrived to help Doctor Cranston establish a clinic, Ackerman saw a chance to make serious money. With a clinic he could order as many drugs as he wanted without creating suspicion. Ackerman even got greedy and began selling drugs to some of the not so good citizens of Grayson. Doctor Cranston became suspicious."

Now it was Cal Markham's turn to laugh. "Cranston brought those suspicions to me. That's when I talked things over with Ackerman."

"You two went into business together," Dehner said. "The first item on the agenda was murder. You killed Doctor Cranston, a fine man."

"Business is business."

"The doctor who will arrive next week will stay in Grayson while Ackerman rides to various small towns and settlements. Ackerman will do enough real doctoring to make it look legitimate, but his real purpose will be to set up clients to sell drugs to and they won't just be saddle bums. There's plenty of folks with money who—"

"Hold it!" The crooked lawman stopped and picked up the pistol belonging to Lang that Dehner had tossed away. He stuck it in his belt on the side opposite Dehner's Colt. "Keep walkin'. We're almost there."

"I've seen army units with less firearms than you have."

"You're a real funny man, Dehner. Keep walkin'."

Dehner continued to talk, in an almost casual manner, hoping Markham would become flustered and blunder into a misstep. "The new doc will certainly be an honest man, or at least a man who doesn't abide turning people into drug addicts. So, handling the drug trade in Grayson will be your job. Ackerman will give you the inventory which you'll hide somewhere and sell to the locals."

They had arrived at Lang's corpse. Markham again ordered Dehner to stop. The crooked lawman looked at the rifle Dehner had kicked away from Lang and used his foot to nudge it closer to the dead outlaw. He then returned Lang's pistol to its holster.

Satisfied with his work, Cal Markham smiled at his captive. "Ya know, more and more stores like Bascomb's are gettin' right fussy 'bout sellin' drugs like morphine, opium and laudanum. There's big talk 'bout makin' 'em illegal. Ackerman and me got a fine future in front of us."

Markham looked at Lang's corpse, then at Dehner. The crooked lawman turned his back to the two trees. He was setting up the scene in his mind, how it would look when outsiders arrived.

Dehner spotted movement behind the trunk of one of the trees. It was Scoop Wilsey. Wilsey looked confused. The detective immediately knew why. Scoop occasionally carried a gun but most of the time he didn't.

This was obviously one of the occasions when he didn't.

Markham carefully took Dehner's Winchester in his left hand and placed it on the ground. "Don't worry, Dehner, I'll be returnin' both guns to ya soon. 'Course ya won't be in any shape to use 'em."

"What exactly do you have in mind, Cal?" Dehner knew exactly what Cal had in mind but was desperately stalling for Scoop to come up with a plan. Even under the circumstances, Dehner understood the newspaperman's dilemma. He was a few yards away. If Wilsey charged at Markham, the lawman would have plenty of time to kill Scoop, then turn and kill the detective.

"Damn, I thought ya was smart, Dehner." Markham spit in the direction of his captive, an obvious insult. "You've already set things up jus' fine. Ya killed Lang. Now, I'm gonna kill you. Folks will think ya two blew each other ta hell in a gunfight."

Rance quickly glanced at the tree and saw nothing. Scoop was doing a great job hiding behind the trunk. He hoped the newspaperman had something a bit more ambitious planned.

The detective came up with one last stall. He

pointed to the rifle lying near the dead outlaw. "Shouldn't you finish me off with that Colt .44 revolving rifle? There's no way anyone would think a bullet from your Sharps-Borschardt came from Lang's gun."

Cal Markham's laughter was loud and genuine. "Ya think I'll fall for that trick?! Hell, Lang's gun could be empty for all I know."

The sheriff's laughter continued. He was enjoying himself. "Besides, ya know who'll examine Lang's body and make the official report? Why, none other than Doctor Edward Ackerman! I ain't too worried 'bout what rifle I use."

The volume of Markham's laughter increased. He didn't hear the scampering sound behind him but felt a lightning bolt of pain as Clyde sank his teeth into the sheriff's leg.

Stunned, Markham let out a tormented yell as he fired at Dehner. The shot went wide and wouldn't have hit the detective even if he hadn't dropped to the ground.

Rance sprang to his feet and ran at Markham. The sheriff was twirling and trying to shake Clyde off his leg. The Sharps-Borschardt was now being employed as a club. Markham took one hard swing, missed the dog but smashed his ankle.

Scoop charged from behind the tree. Dehner arrived first. He grabbed Cal Markham's rifle and used it as a club against the crooked lawman's head. Markham crumpled to the ground, semi-conscious.

Satisfied his task was completed, Clyde let go of Markham's leg. Scoop crouched over Clyde and began to pet him, "Good dog, good dog!"

Rance glanced briefly at the newspaperman. "You and Clyde saved my life."

"Clyde gets the credit," Scoop gave the dog a final ear scratch, then stood up. "The dog usually stays closer to Mandy than to me but when I rode out of town, he must have sensed I would be needing him."

"I'm sure glad he did." Rance kept Markham's rifle pointed at Markham. He used his foot to scoot the Winchester a safe distance away. He jerked the two pistols from Markham's belt, handed his Colt to Scoop and tossed the other gun. It landed beside the Winchester. As a precaution, Dehner wanted both weapons far away from his prisoner until Markham was tied up and helpless.

A nervousness suddenly came into Scoop Wilsey's voice and gestures. The tension he had kept submerged was surfacing. "Behind the tree, I tried to explain to Clyde that he should attack Cal Markham. Wasn't that tough. Clyde never cared much for that guy."

Scoop looked at the sheriff, now lying on the ground, his head and leg bleeding. Then he looked at Clyde who was panting and smiling, obviously aware of his hero status. "I'm sure glad Clyde wasn't injured. Mandy would never have forgiven me."

"Do you think Mandy is more concerned with Clyde's health than with keeping you and me alive?"

Scoop gave his friend a whimsical smile. "Just be glad she won't have to answer the question."

"Where's your horse?" Rance asked.

Scoop pointed backwards with his thumb. "Behind the tree."

"Do you have a rope?"

"Sure do, and I'll fetch it right now."

When Wilsey returned with his horse, Cal Markham was sitting up. A bandanna had been tied around his head. Rance was crouched beside him. "I think I've stopped his head from bleeding," Rance said. "I'll ask your wife to take a closer look when we get back to town. Doctor Ackerman won't be available."

The newspaperman chuckled as he removed the rope from his saddle and carried it over to Dehner. "We'll have to take the prisoner in by ourselves. I tried to talk Buck into getting up a posse, but he wouldn't do it. He explained he needed to stay in town, along with Fancy Pants, as he calls Stacey. Buck seemed content to let the sheriff and you catch up with the hired killer. It was my idea to follow you."

Rance nodded as he began to tie Markham's hands in front of him. "I told Buck and Stacey my suspicions about Ackerman. I still wasn't sure about the sheriff, so I kept my mouth shut."

Rance stood up from his crouch. "I'll hold the end of the rope as we ride back into Grayson. I don't think Cal will give us much trouble. He's barely conscious."

"I heard much of your conversation with our esteemed sheriff, Rance. I never dreamed all of these killings related to selling drugs."

Dehner gave his friend a wide smile. "I suspect you'll be up late tonight working on tomorrow's *Grayson Herald*."

"I may provide my readers with more confusion than light."

"What do you mean?"

Scoop pushed his hat back and scratched his head as if trying to bring up the right question. "How would killing Mack Wong help Markham and the good doctor sell drugs on a mass scale?"

"There was never any plan to kill Mack Wong."

The newspaperman looked stunned. "I don't—"

"Sammy Wong was always the target," Rance explained. "Sammy hated people who sold drugs for the wrong reason. He would eventually catch on to what Ackerman and Markham were doing."

"But,—"

Rance looked at his prisoner. The man's head seemed to still be bleeding slightly and lines of blood continued to run down his leg. The detective didn't much care. He pointed down at the crooked sheriff. "This coyote knew that if Sammy Wong were killed directly, a lot of folks would be curious as to why. A U.S. Marshal would probably get involved."

A knowing expression slapped across Scoop's face. "So, the sheriff and the doctor created a false story about a group of bigots who hated Asians and were out to kill Mack Wong, the fighter known as the Dragon, who had already knocked out plenty of white fighters and was now taking on Bill Connors."

"Correct!" Dehner beamed approval. "Let's see if you can get the rest of it."

"Doctor Ackerman arranged for that so called celebration in the Mule Kick. He made sure Mack Wong was sitting right beside his Uncle Sammy Wong."

"Right," Rance continued. "And he hired a professional to kill Sammy. It had to look like Mack Wong was the real target. Sammy had to be killed by accident."

Cal Markham mumbled a few profanities. Rance and Scoop laughed derisively.

"Markham and Ackerman have been using the town fools as henchmen," Dehner said. "When Jeb killed Lang, they'd have a dead scapegoat."

Scoop nodded. "They'd probably have claimed that the scapegoat also killed Doctor Cranston."

Markham's voice rose above a mumble. "All Ackerman's idea, I . . ."

The sheriff's words became jumbled and senseless. His captors didn't really care.

"Scoop, can you keep an eye on this snake for a moment?"

The journalist held up the Colt Rance had handed him. "Sure."

"I need to retrieve my horse and the one belonging to Markham. We have to get back to town soon." Rance turned and ran toward the stream.

Chapter Twenty-Seven

Stacey Hooper and Edward Ackerman each had one of Jeb Smith's arms around his shoulder as they helped the bartender into the doctor's surgery. Ackerman used his head as a pointer to the large table in the middle of the room. "Let's dump him there."

Smith cursed in a voice both angry and weak.

Stacey rebuked the prisoner. "Do try to show more gratitude, Jeb! After all, you were shot while trying to shoot Rance Dehner, an outstanding citizen. Fortunately for you, civilization is coming to the West. Two decades back you would have been left to bleed to death in the dust. This is definitely a time to count your blessings."

Smith's second round of vulgarities was louder and saltier as he was laid down flat on the table.

"Thanks for the assistance, Mr. Hooper," Ackerman said. "You best get back to helping Buck. What with Dehner and the sheriff taking off after that gunman, the deputy will probably be needing help to keep the town under control."

"Indeed. And I'm sure you can handle any problems our wounded bartender may present."

Ackerman nodded assent, then watched Stacey leave the room. The doctor walked to the other side of the room and pushed a cart containing various medical supplies to the table where his patient lay. Anger laced his voice as he picked up a pair of scissors and began to cut Smith's shirt. "The bullet only grazed your side, you'll be okay."

"I'm bleeding."

"It's your own damn fault! Why didn't you spot Dehner in the alley right across from you?"

Jeb looked away from Ackerman and stared at the ceiling. He didn't really want to see his injury or what the doctor was doing to it. "I did what you tole me. I hid behind the rain barrel. When I heard a shot, I was supposed to stand up and shoot Lang, so you wouldn't have to pay him the rest of his money. I couldn't see Dehner from behind the barrel, didn't know he was around 'til I heard him shout at Lang."

Anger once again flared in Ackerman's voice as he tended to the patient. "You were going to be a big hero: the man who gunned down the outlaw who killed Sammy Wong by mistake and was about to put a bullet in Mack. A vicious killer who probably disposed of Doc Cranston. We could have used you to help Markham get drugs to the customers in Grayson."

Jeb Smith grimaced in pain as a medication was applied to his side. "I am a damn hero. I organized people like Boone Witter. We were right there for you when you needed us to make it look like someone wanted to kill the Dragon. It was me who got Witter to charge the church with a torch. Hell, he wouldn't even have gone there to cause a ruckus if I hadn't gone with him. And I was in charge of them three that kidnapped the girl. I took real chances for you and Markham. Dehner almost caught me when he rescued the girl . . ."

Ackerman laughed derisively as he finished bandaging the wound.

"What's so damn funny?"

"Those jaspers you claim to have organized did what they did for the free drugs I provided." The doctor sighed heavily as he left the patient and headed for a wall cabinet. "I'll admit, matters did get out of hand. The laudanum made Jeff Taggert a total moron. He'd cause trouble for no reason, at the drop of a hat. I couldn't control him."

Smith watched the doctor anxiously, then his face brightened as he watched Ackerman take a small bottle of laudanum out of the cabinet. His voice now carried excitement. "I figgered you gave the poison to Arnie. You couldn't be sure what he might say."

Edward Ackerman carried the bottle over to his patient. "Yep. But I figure most folks will blame the old chink bird for it. I thought the young gal would bring the soup over but the old bird works out even better."

Jeb opened the bottle and drank the contents. "We gotta come up with a way to git rid of that whole no-good family. I spotted that chink whore leavin' the church with a white man Wednesday night. She had the fool eatin' outta her hand. Think what kinda kids those two would have!"

The kids issue obviously didn't interest Edward Ackerman. "Rest up some. I'll give you another couple bottles of laudanum before you leave tonight."

"Leave for where?"

"That part's up to you. Of course, the official story will be that you escaped. But you must get out of Grayson. After today, you're no good to us."

"You can't just run me off!"

"You prefer to go to jail?!" Ackerman shouted. "Everyone knows you fired at a detective."

Smith's voice became accusatory. "Look, Ackerman, you and the sheriff is real good at making up stories. So, come up with a good reason why I tried to shoot Dehner. Hell, Markham can kill the damn detective easy enough, jus' like he killed Kendrick."

"Would you care for a little whiskey to go with the laudanum?"

Jeb took the offer as a surrender. "Sure, Doc, thanks for the hospitality."

Ackerman returned to the cabinet where he kept the drugs. But instead of a whiskey bottle he brought down a Smith and Wesson revolver.

"You know, Jeb, it's probably best this way. What I said about laudanum drinkers not lasting long is true. You'd probably be dead in less than a year. And, let me assure you, finding another source to sustain your bad habit would be very difficult."

Jeb began to sputter his words. "People will know you—"

Ackerman's back was to the door of his office. He didn't notice it opening. "People will know I killed a violent man—"

Stacey Hooper's voice cut in from the doorway. "No need to work your imagination any further, Doctor. Drop the gun or I will be obligated to use mine."

Edward Ackerman froze. He had already killed for his dream of riches. That dream was close to being destroyed. But by taking a quick, crazy chance maybe he could save it yet.

Buck's voice now sounded behind him. "Better do what he says, Doc. It's all over."

Maybe it isn't over, Ackerman thought. Jeb is no problem. All that stands in my way is a limey and an old man.

The doctor began a fast pivot toward the open door. As he did, he momentarily lifted his gun hand upward. Stacey fired and sparks seemed to propel out of Ackerman's hand. A sharp whine sounded through the room. Ackerman yelled in shock as his gun hand was forced backwards.

The weapon lurched from his palm and spun in the air before hitting the floor.

"I don't believe it!" Buck pushed past Stacey and ran toward the Smith and Wesson that now lay hopelessly damaged.

"You shot the gun outta his hand, Fancy Pants!" Something between awe and disbelief filled the deputy's face. "Jus' like one of them dime novel fellers."

For a moment, Stacey Hooper stood in a stunned silence. In his shock he almost revealed that he had been aiming at the doctor's shoulder. But the gambler quickly composed himself. "Of course! There have been enough people shot already!" he declared, his voice ringing with nobleness.

Hooper grimaced. He had been trying for something more elevated. Maybe he should have employed a quote from Shakespeare. But he couldn't bring up anything appropriate to the moment.

Doctor Ackerman was looking at his hand. Jeb Smith stared at the empty bottle of laudanum as if it told him something significant about his life. Buck realized there was work that needed to be done.

The deputy looked to the man he called Fancy Pants. "We better git these two jaspers ta jail." He pointed at the floor. "Meanwhile, we'll leave the gun right where it is."

Stacey was still in awe over his achievement. "Why?"

"Scoop will wanna take a picture of it," Buck answered. "You're gonna be on the front page of the newspaper, Fancy Pants!"

Chapter Twenty-Eight

Buck stood nervously in the living room of Sammy Wong's home. Sammy was perched comfortably in his favorite chair. His sister-in-law, Wai Lan, was sitting in a chair beside him. As always, her posture was perfect and her face pleasant but unreadable.

"Thank you for come here, Buck, so sorry lazy mayor must be brought up to date on events in town he is supposed to be administering." Sammy's good natured humor was aimed more at making Buck feel at ease than making him laugh.

Buck smiled nervously and twirled his hat in his hand.

"Please take seat, Buck." The mayor pointed to a chair directly across from his.

Buck sat down and continued to twirl his hat.

Sammy smiled broadly. "You have had very busy day. Please explain what mayor should know."

Buck stopped looking at his hat and looked at Sammy Wong. "Things is pretty crazy. I got Doc Ackerman and the sheriff locked up. Jeb Smith, too. That barkeep is gonna be a big help when the circuit judge gits here in ten days."

"Why do you say that?" Sammy asked.

"Jeb is singin' like a bird at sunrise, even when

the truth don't make him look so good. Your barkeep was the one what left that letter for ya, threatenin' to kill Mack. It was also Jeb who beat up Scoop in that alley last Tuesday night."

"Did Jeb Smith arrange kidnap of my daughter?"

"Jeb didn't arrange nothin'. Everthin' that's been happenin' was thought up by Ackerman and Markham. The doc mostly. But, yep, Jeb had a hand in grabbin' your daughter. It was him that knocked it all off track."

"How so?"

"The plan was for Jeb and three other worthless barflies to grab your daughter, ride off and take her to the old Carson place. Cal Markham was to ride out alone after them. When he got to the Carson place, he was s'pose ta yell for the owlhoots to turn the girl loose. They would do it and then vamoose like they was scared of the sheriff."

"The point of this charade was more effort to make everyone think Mack Wong is target of killers, not humble self." Sammy made a funny face and pointed to himself as he said, "humble self."

Buck's chuckle was genuine and he relaxed a bit. "Yeh. But Jeb blew that scheme to . . . hades. To make the whole kidnappin' look real, he fired wide at the sheriff. But the bullet bounced off a rock and hit Cal's leg, puttin' him out for the night. With the sheriff gone, those jaspers got some pretty awful ideas, but . . ."

"But very fortunate, you, Rance Dehner, and Stacey Hooper rescue daughter. You have forever the gratitude of self and family."

Buck once again looked at this hat.

Sammy continued. "Buck, I ask you to please be Sheriff of Grayson. You are best man for job. I also ask you, kindly select worthy deputy."

Buck tossed his hat a few inches into the air and caught it before speaking. "I'll take the job, temporary. I'll find a young fella who'll make a good lawman. The next election for sheriff is still two years away. He'll be ready plenty by then. After that, I'll stay on ta help iffen he wants."

"Thank you, Buck, you are valuable man to town and old mayor."

Buck looked nervously at Wai Lan. "Ma'am, there is a reason I asked the mayor to include you in our meeting."

Wai Lan smiled politely. "Yes, Sheriff?"

Buck looked confused, then realized the woman's use of "sheriff" applied to him. He smiled, nodded his head, then continued. "Doc Ackerman poisoned Jeff Taggert. We know that now. But I always knowed ya had nothin' to do with it and so did anybody else that's got any sense."

He pressed his lips together, his face flushed red in either embarrassment, anger, or both.

"Most folks in Grayson is good, but we got our bad apples. I sure am sorry ya had ta listen ta some of the ugly names that got throwed at ya."

Sammy was surprised by the warmth which encompassed Wai Lan's face. His sister-in-law rarely displayed such emotions in public.

The woman spoke softly. "Thank you, Sheriff, but there is no need for apologize. I know people such as yourself are much more representative of Grayson."

The sheriff's face reddened even more, "Appreciate it, ma'am." He rose from the chair. "Well, I best git back ta work right now, the town's in the hands of Rance Dehner and Fancy Pants . . . ah . . . that Hooper fella."

Sammy and Wai Lan exchanged smiles as Buck awkwardly made his way out of the room. When she was alone with her brother-in-law Wai Lan's smile turned wistful. "So, some people thought I kill man with poison."

"Do not worry, whole story soon come out in the newspaper. People will know the truth."

"The truth is I did kill with poison."

Sammy's face seemed to expand in shock. "You didn't kill Arnie!"

"No," Wai Lan gently replied. "But I poisoned your brother. I kill the Dragon."

A tremor passed through Wai Lan's body. She sat in silence for a moment and then began to speak while staring straight ahead. "The Bit Wong

I knew at first was kind and generous. I very young and not wise of the world to understand he was taking drugs, also working for drug lords. I learned all about it when he abandon me and my son, Munchoo, who you now call Mack."

"But if he left you, how—"

"After six years, my husband suddenly come back one night. He just walk in the door, order me to call him 'the Dragon' and ask about Munchoo, who was stay with friends."

"Did Bit tell you what he had been doing?"

"No. The Dragon say he would be oversee a group of opium dens. He spoke with pride, as if the job was important position with great company." Still staring straight ahead, the woman laughed in a strange manner. "Perhaps that is how he thought of it."

"Did Bit plan to move back in with you?"

"Yes, but he had little interest in me. He keep asking about Munchoo. My son is only eight at the time. I know he would soon come to worship father and follow his path. The Dragon was man who naturally inspire devotion. I poison him same night. Munchoo never know his father returned."

"How did you get rid of the body?"

"Friends did this work for me. You need not know all details. I did awful thing. Perhaps you should turn me over to new sheriff. I could become one more task for judge."

Sammy wasn't sure if the woman was joking or not. He spoke in a low, intense voice. "You did awful thing, but also right thing. Son you raise is testimony to your wisdom." Sammy paused, then continued. "Have you spoken of this matter with anyone else?"

"No."

"Do not speak of it again. The past can now only bring great sadness to your son."

The woman nodded her head. "You are correct. What I have done has already brought great sadness to me. I will continue to carry sadness for the rest of life."

"Wai Lan, tomorrow morning come with us to church. The pastor, Paul Colten, is a man who can speak with you about forgiveness—"

"No!" Wai Lan stood up. "I murdered husband and deserve to suffer all my life for such treacherous act. I do not seek forgiveness in this world or next." She left the room.

Chapter Twenty-Nine

The Sunday service had been over for a good hour and the congregation was just departing. Folks had stayed around to shake hands and chat with Mack Wong and Bill Connors, both of whom had been in attendance.

As the crowd departed, a small group of people huddled in front of the church. They were people who had just been through dangerous times together and realized those times were over. Some of them might never see each other again.

Preacher Paul smiled at the man who had just been the primary center of attention. "How much longer will you stay in Grayson, Mack?"

"We are leaving tomorrow," Mack answered. "My mother, Barry Thomas, Bill Connors and I all have tickets on the noon stagecoach."

Bruiser Bill noticed the surprise on everyone's face. "Mack has agreed to give this washed up boxer a job."

"I am starting a small detective agency in San Francisco," Mack explained. "It will only deal with problems in Chinatown. Bill may not know language of Chinatown but I can testify that his fists communicate well in any language."

Paul chortled along with everyone else, then

gave Peter Thomas a crooked smile. “I noticed you are staying with us, Peter.”

“Yes, Preacher, I have an appointment tomorrow morning at the bank. I’m purchasing the old Carson place and turning it into a horse ranch.”

For a moment, loud expressions of approval filled the air. But the well-wishes were all laced with a prodding nature. More information was desired. Sammy Wong addressed the unspoken question. “Mr. Peter Thomas and daughter talk about making another announcement soon. But humble self have doubts. When Peter learn true nature of future father-in-law, he may skip town.”

This time, laughter filled the air. Jenny’s face flushed red as her eyes did a careful inspection of the ground.

Mandy hurriedly changed the subject. “Rance, how did you peg Doctor Ackerman as being the one behind all these threats and killings?”

“Ackerman’s weakness was his hired help,” Dehner answered. “They were drug addicts and except for Jeb, almost out of control. The good doctor was afraid Buck might figure out that Edward Ackerman was the source of all the wild men in town. So, Ackerman handed Buck a story about laudanum being stolen from Bascomb’s Emporium. It was a lie.”

“Ackerman’s attempt at deception got my friend’s able brain moving in a certain direction,”

Stacey explained. "I assisted by pointing out that Ackerman lacked the temperament for all the violence his scheme demanded. He had to have an accomplice."

Scoop Wilsey instinctively reached into his coat pocket for a notebook that wasn't there. He asked a question anyway. "How did you figure Cal Markham as the number two man, Rance?"

"The sheriff seemed very uncomfortable with you trying to probe into Doctor Cranston's murder, Scoop. He was afraid you'd come to suspect the real reason why Doctor Cranston was killed. There was another matter. On the night Boone Witter was killed while firing at Paul and then trying to set fire to the church, the sheriff led Stacey and me as we were running toward the church. He started firing much too soon to do any good. I suspected he was signaling the other gunman to ride off."

"And he was also quick 'bout shootin' down Jeff Taggert," Buck chimed in.

"Yes," Rance agreed. "I suspect Cal gave Taggert a Derringer when he ran into the dark alley to get him, after Taggert hit the wall and plunged to the ground. A drug addict doesn't plan far ahead. Unlikely that Jeff Taggert carried a concealed Derringer just in case he might need it. Cal told Taggert to wait for the right moment, then use it to escape. Taggert was an easy target for the sheriff to manipulate."

"Cal always carried a Derringer in his belt," Buck added. "Ya done some good thinkin', Rance. But none of what ya said would be worth a thimble full of spit in court."

Dehner nodded in agreement. "Yes. So, I kept my thoughts about the sheriff private."

"Time now for celebration," Sammy exclaimed. "All of you invited to home of humble self for evening meal."

The response was cheerful and positive except for Rance Dehner. "Thank you, Sammy, but my friend and I need to leave for Dallas soon."

Walking back to the hotel, Stacey observed, "You seem a tad melancholy, good friend. There is a certain quality to Grayson which makes one think of putting down roots . . . and all that. Do you wish Grayson could be your permanent environs?"

"Maybe. There's something about the Wong family, the way they help each other. At times they almost function as a unit. I can't help but think—"

"You must purge all such thoughts," Hooper declared. "Detectives, like gamblers, were never intended for the home fires. Justice, like victory in cards, is a taskmaster that always beckons you to new horizons."

Dehner smiled and tried to act cheerful as they picked up their belongings at the hotel, then saddled up and began to ride out of town. They would allow their horses a relaxed pace. A long trip lay ahead.

Dehner felt himself tense up as they approached the office of the *Grayson Herald*. He privately confessed to himself that Mandy and Scoop Wilsey had achieved something in life he wanted and increasingly suspected he would never have. The two newspaper people were like the Wongs; they had a home in the deepest sense of the word.

As they passed the office, Rance could spot Mandy and Scoop inside. He waved to them, but they were busy and didn't notice.

Stacey Hooper sensed that his friend's spirits were low. He remained uncharacteristically silent as the two men rode out of Grayson, Texas.

Center Point Large Print
600 Brooks Road / PO Box 1
Thorndike, ME 04986-0001 USA

(207) 568-3717

US & Canada:
1 800 929-9108
www.centerpointlargeprint.com